THE POWER AND THE PRINCE

Prince Ivan's words were passionate, unyielding, yet Alana allowed herself no surrender.

"Love is something that cannot be denied, cannot be refused," Ivan protested, "though I thought the real ecstasy and wonder of it was something that would never exist for me."

At last Alana's strength gave way. "But I cannot . . . marry you," she sobbed.

"Then tell me why!" the Prince insisted. "And hurry, my precious, say what you have to say, before I take you in my arms. You are mine, Alana, mine since the beginning of time, and mine for the rest of eternity, and whether you marry me or not, that is an indisputable fact!"

Bantam Books by Barbara Cartland
Ask your bookseller for the books you have missed

Barbara Cartland's Library of Love series

THE MONEY MOON
ONLY A GIRL'S LOVE

Books of Love and Revelation

THE TREASURE OF HO

Other Books by Barbara Cartland

I SEEK THE MIRACULOUS

The Power
and
the Prince

Barbara Cartland

BANTAM BOOKS
TORONTO · NEW YORK · LONDON

THE POWER AND THE PRINCE
A Bantam Book / March 1980

ISBN 0–553–13570–8

Published simultaneously in the United States and Canada

Bantam Books are published by Bantam Books, Inc. Its trade-
mark, consisting of the words "Bantam Books" and the por-
trayal of a bantam, is Registered in U.S. Patent and Trademark
Office and in other countries. Marca Registrada. Bantam
Books, Inc., 666 Fifth Avenue, New York, New York 10019.

PRINTED IN THE UNITED STATES OF AMERICA

Author's Note

The Russian or rather the Slavic nation has defied adequate description all down the centuries, although many writers have tried. The magnetism, the luminous spiritual force, is linked with dramatic exaltation and excess. Love to a Russian comes from *Drouska*—the Soul, usually the *suffering* soul.

The Russian peasants sang songs of their suffering not of the body, as might be expected, but of their souls. Love and pain are intermingled until it is impossible to separate them.

Russians are a blend of despair and optimism, grandiose schemes and sheer futility, superb idealism and wild excess. They can become maddened and intoxicated by misery or exalted by love into an ecstasy in which they are one with God.

The greatest change in Tzar Alexander II's reign, after the liberation of the Serfs, was the "reduced circumstances" of the Secret Police. Under his predecessor, the tyrannical Tzar Nicholas I—"the most alarming Sovereign in Europe"— Universities were put under Police supervision, foreign travel was prohibited, public meetings were banned, and soldiers were sent to Siberia for nothing more serious than a button out-of-place.

Chapter One

1878

Lady Odele Ashford, settled comfortably in a private carriage attached to the main-line train, thought with satisfaction that she would soon be reaching the Halt near Charl.

Exceedingly lovely in her sables and a travelling-gown that was very elegant, as she stared out the window she looked exactly like her photographs which appeared in many shop-windows and proclaimed her one of the great beauties of the period.

She was looking particularly attractive at the moment because she was thinking of what lay ahead of her and that she would see Prince Ivan again and undoubtedly, for a few hours at any rate, alone.

His letter had been explicit when he had asked her to come to Charl early before the rest of his house-party arrived.

When she thought of his handsome face, his dark passionate eyes, and his slim athletic body, Lady Odele fancied that her heart beat more quickly and

1

she was conscious of some new sensations in that vacillating organ.

She told herself that it was a long time since she had had a lover so attractive, so eloquent in his love-making, and above all so rich.

Even amongst the very wealthy members of Society who clustered round the Prince of Wales at Marlborough House, the fortune of Prince Ivan was greater, Lady Odele had heard her husband say, than that of all the rest put together.

The fact that he had singled her out of all the numerous beautiful women who pursued him relentlessly made it seem all the more flattering.

Prince Ivan in inviting her to stay this particular week at Charl had chosen his moment well.

He would not have been unaware that Edward Ashford, whose only real love was horses, would be racing at Doncaster, and although there was every likelihood of his joining his wife when the races were over, she would be on her own for at least two days, perhaps three.

What was there about Prince Ivan, Lady Odele asked herself, that made him so irresistible and very much more intriguing than all the good-looking Englishmen whom she met night after night at Marlborough House and in all the great houses where parties were continually being held for the Prince of Wales?

She supposed it was partly his Russian ancestry, even though he was half-English, but Lady Odele considered it was more than that.

The Prince was so intelligent that, she was told, even the most distinguished Statesmen bowed to his superior knowledge when it came to politics.

He was also listened to with respect on many other subjects when the men sat round the Dining-Room table enjoying their port after the ladies had left the room.

2

That he was an outstanding rider and that his judgement of horse-flesh kept him winning all the Classic races, to the envy of her infuriated husband and other members of the Jockey Club, went without saying.

Besides all that, there was, she decided, something mysterious about him, something which women found intriguing and to which they searched for the key, only to be disappointed.

But whatever it might be, Lady Odele told herself that she was looking forward with an almost girlish excitement to arriving at Charl.

The train was slowing down and now she could see the Halt, at which there was a notice reading:

CHARL CASTLE ONLY

Waiting, as she expected, were the Prince's servants in their distinctive livery and the Prince's private secretary in a bowler hat.

There was a red carpet laid along the platform, and Lady Odele knew that outside would be waiting an extremely comfortable carriage drawn by four magnificent horses which would carry her to the Castle at a speed which would leave most people breathless.

The train stopped but she made no attempt to move until the door was opened and she saw the Prince's secretary bowing to her, hat in hand, and her lady's-maid had emerged from the next carriage and was waiting with her sable muff.

With a smile that Lady Odele used automatically to enslave every man and woman on whom she bestowed it, she stepped out onto the platform.

"Welcome to Charl, My Lady!" Mr. Brothwick, the Prince's secretary, said.

"Thank you," Lady Odele replied, and with the grace of a swan moved along the red carpet towards the entrance of the Halt.

3

She was well aware that all the windows in the train were filled with faces eager to see one of the renowned beauties of England.

Because she never disappointed what she secretly called "her public," she turned round deliberately to speak to her maid, who was following behind her, so that those watching would have a glimpse of her fabulous pink-and-white skin, her blue eyes, and her golden hair.

"You have not forgotten my jewel-case, Robinson?"

It was quite an unnecessary question as Robinson was holding it tightly with both hands.

"No, M'Lady."

Lady Odele glanced at the train as if she had never seen it before, and thought she could almost hear the "Ooh's" and "Aah's" of admiration her movement evoked.

Then she turned to leave the station and was helped into the luxurious carriage that was waiting for her.

It was only two miles to Charl and Lady Odele did not trouble to bend forward, as new visitors to the great Castle always did, as it appeared standing above the valley, its hundreds of windows flashing in the sunlight, its great tower surmounted with a flag.

Lady Odele had in fact known Charl for many years.

Because she was fond of Lord Charlwood, to whose family it had belonged for four centuries, she had been glad for his sake when Prince Ivan had bought it from him and proceeded to spend a fortune on redecorating the interior.

Although it must have been hard to part with something which meant so much to the Charlwood family, the money the Prince had paid for it meant that the sixth Lord Charlwood and his wife could continue to live the gay social life they enjoyed without getting further and further into debt.

One of the largest houses in England, Charl was, Lady Odele thought, a perfect setting for Prince Ivan, and she had wondered in the past why, when he spent so much time in the country where his mother had been born, he did not have a house of his own here.

It was true that he had houses all over Europe, a Palazzo in Venice, a *Château* in France, a Shooting-Lodge in Hungary, and a Villa in Monte Carlo, where Lady Odele had already determined she must be a guest next spring.

But first she knew that Prince Ivan was planning several large-scale pheasant-shoots at Charl to amuse the Prince of Wales, where he could also hunt with two of the best packs in the Midlands.

She was sure too that there would be numerous large and small Balls in the great Ball-Room, where she would shine like a glittering star.

Lady Odele was so intent on her thoughts that she was almost surprised when she realised the carriage was already turning in to the great gravel sweep which lay in front of the Castle.

She had a quick glance at herself in a little mirror which she carried in her handbag and saw that her nose needed no more powder and her lips were as red as they dared to be.

She was aware that she exuded an exotic French perfume every time she moved, and the huge spray of purple orchids which had been waiting for her in the carriage when she arrived at King's Cross looked very elegant pinned to her many-tailed sable wrap.

There were six footmen waiting on the steps as she proceeded up them, and the Butler, looking like a pontifical Archbishop, was waiting in the Hall.

"Welcome back to Charl, M'Lady!" he said with

the same tone of sincerity that Mr. Brothwick had used.

"Thank you, Newton," Lady Odele replied. "It is delightful to be back again."

"His Highness is waiting for you in the Blue Salon, M'Lady."

Lady Odele smiled secretly to herself.

She knew that the Blue Salon, which was one of the smaller rooms at Charl, was part of the Prince's private apartments and no guests ever encroached on it unless specially invited.

As she moved, she was conscious of the silk petticoats of her bustle rustling behind her, and she was glad that because it was still warm for the beginning of October, she had not been obliged to wear one of her thicker travelling-gowns.

The thinner one she had on was made of a material that clung to her fabulous figure and was warm enough, as over it she wore her famous sables.

These had been given to her by a rich man who loved her passionately, but they did not compare in value to a stole and muff made of chinchilla, which she had already determined should be one of the Prince's gifts to her.

She reached the door of the Blue Salon and Newton announced with a flourish:

"Lady Odele Ashford, Your Highness!"

The Prince, who had been reading a newspaper, rose as she entered, and now Lady Odele was quite certain that her heart was beating quicker than usual.

It was always the same when she saw the Prince; again she found that she had forgotten how handsome he was and how his dark eyes, which could glow with a passionate fire or appear cynical and slightly mocking, had that penetrating look which seemed to search into the innermost secrets of a woman's soul.

"Ivan!"

The word was an exclamation of joy, and he

moved towards her with a grace that was untypical of Englishmen and lifted her hand to his lips.

He kissed her glove conventionally, then with his eyes holding hers captive he drew the soft suede from her hand and kissed her palm.

She felt herself quiver at the warm insistence of his lips. He drew her across the room to the sofa by the fire and sat down beside her.

"How are you? You have had a comfortable journey?" he asked. "You were properly looked after?"

His voice was deep and seductive, and as he spoke his eyes flickered over her, taking in every detail, Lady Odele thought, of her face, her gown, and the orchids he had given her.

"Everything was perfect, as it always is when you have arranged it."

"You look very lovely!"

That was what she wanted him to say and she smiled at him beguilingly.

He sat looking at her. Part of his fascination, she thought, was that he was unlike any other man who by this time would have been fondling and kissing her.

He was controlled and the very waiting for his favours made them, when they came, more exciting.

"Why did you want me to arrive before the rest of the party?"

She told herself that she really should wait until he chose his own time to tell her why. At the same time, she was extremely curious and she could not prevent herself from asking the obvious question.

"You know that I wanted to see you," Prince Ivan replied.

Lady Odele gave a little sigh of satisfaction.

"We have at least two days, and even then Edward may find something on four legs more amusing than joining me."

The Prince laughed.

"Then we will be very happy together," he said,

"and I have planned many amusements for my guests while, as you well know, the one thing which will amuse me will be—you."

"Dear Ivan!" Lady Odele said caressingly. "That is what I wanted you to say."

"I expect you would like to change after your journey. We will have tea in here and afterwards I want to talk to you."

Lady Odele raised her eye-brows.

"Talk?"

"After tea."

He rose as he spoke, and Lady Odele knew there would be no use asking questions, no use doing anything but exactly what he wished.

It was undoubtedly one of his strange holds over women, that he commanded and they obeyed. He knew exactly what he wanted and did not allow his plans to be changed by anyone.

He took her to the door. Outside, the Groom-of-the-Chambers was waiting and Lady Odele found herself being escorted to her bedroom, where already her maid was unpacking the trunks which had been carried upstairs.

It was nearly an hour later, for Lady Odele was not able to change quickly, when she returned to the Blue Salon, wearing one of the exquisite gowns that were designed especially for her by the great Frederick Worth.

It had a bustle in a waterfall of gathered satin and frilled chiffon which made her look not like a swan but an exotic Bird-of-Paradise. Her fair hair haloed her Grecian-shaped head and its curled fringe was like a wave above her arched eye-brows.

Very conscious of her beauty, she moved towards the tea-table that had been set on the hearth-rug, where the Prince, standing in front of the fire, was watching her appreciatively.

'He loves me,' she thought complacently.

She had found, as she expected, that the bedroom allotted to her was in the same wing of the Castle as his private suite.

She poured out the China tea, knowing, as she did so, that her hands with their long white fingers were being shown to advantage.

"You have the best tea I have ever tasted anywhere," she remarked, "but then, Ivan, everything concerned with you is the best, and no-one can argue about that."

"That is what I wish it to be," the Prince said. "I thought to myself as you came across the room that there is nobody in England who has your grace and beauty."

Lady Odele smiled.

"I doubt that the Prince of Wales would agree with you. He is completely besotted by Mrs. Langtry."

"I am aware of that," the Prince replied. "His Royal Highness and Lillie will be arriving tomorrow."

"You did not tell me this was to be a Royal party!" Lady Odele exclaimed.

"I did not say it was not," the Prince answered.

She knew she had made a mistake in expecting him to discuss his guests, or anything else that concerned him personally, with anyone, not even with her.

"I am of course delighted that they are both coming," she said quickly. "I like Mrs. Langtry, even though most women are extremely jealous of her."

She looked at the Prince from under her eyelashes as she spoke, and added:

"And I too shall be very jealous of her, Ivan, if you find her more attractive than I."

The Prince did not reply that it was impossible. He merely smiled somewhat enigmatically, and Lady Odele went on:

9

"I shall console myself with the knowledge that most of the women you have liked have been fair. It is, of course, the attraction of opposites."

She glanced at the Prince's dark, shining head as she spoke, and she thought that despite the fact that his mother had been English, everything about his appearance was Russian.

The Prince put his cup and saucer down on the table and said:

"Now, I want to talk to you, Odele. I want your help."

"My help?" Lady Odele echoed in surprise.

She had been wondering all the time she was changing what he wished to talk to her about, but, try as she might, she could not imagine for one moment what it could possibly be.

Although he had asked her to arrive early so that they could be alone, she had not imagined it was because he wished to "make love" to her before the rest of his guests arrived.

She was aware that the Prince would not accept the discomfort of making love on a sofa in the afternoon, in imitation of the Prince of Wales and a number of other gentlemen who inevitably copied his example.

This was necessary only because at that time of the day the husband of the lady in question was usually at his Club and the lovers were unlikely to be disturbed.

But such clandestine difficulties were quite unnecessary when Lady Odele was sleeping conveniently near to the Prince's suite and they would have the night ahead of them.

Therefore, his desire to see her at tea-time, Lady Odele was sure, did not concern their love for each other.

But what else could it be?

She had racked her brains for an explanation not

only on the train but almost every minute since she had arrived at Charl, and had found no answer.

Now she moved from behind the tea-table to sit in a more favourable light by the window, aware, as she did so, that her movements, her hair, and the discreet glitter of diamonds in her ears were all exceedingly alluring.

"You know, dearest Ivan," she said softly, "if I can help you I am always ready to do so, but I cannot imagine what it can be. You have made me curious to know in what way it is possible for me to be of assistance."

"That is what I am going to tell you," the Prince said, "and you know, Odele, that because we mean so much to each other, you are the only person whose advice I would ask in this particular difficulty."

Lady Odele draped her hands elegantly on one side of her lap and raised her blue eyes in an attitude of almost child-like attention.

It seemed to her as if the Prince was feeling for words. Then with his usual determined, unhesitating manner, which was mitigated by the depth of fascination of his voice, he said:

"My wife died last week."

Lady Odele was startled.

She had forgotten the Prince's wife, as everybody else had.

The Princess was never mentioned, but now that she thought of her, Lady Odele remembered that she had been Hungarian and had been injured many years ago, soon after they were married, in a riding-accident.

It was averred, although the Prince never spoke of her, that she was in fact mad and was shut up in a Nursing-Home in Hungary.

"It was of course a merciful release," the Prince said quietly. "She had not recognised anyone for years,

11

and it would be pointless to pretend that even her closest relatives will mourn her death."

"So you are free!" Lady Odele said softly.

It flashed through her mind that the Prince might be making her a proposal of marriage. Then she knew that even to think of such a thing was quite ridiculous.

However outrageously those in the Social World behaved in private, there was one commandment they always obeyed, one hard and fast rule that was never broken:

"Thou shalt not cause a scandal!"

Odele knew that even if the Prince went down on his knees and offered her himself and everything he possessed, she would refuse without even a moment's hesitation.

However much she loved a man, and she told herself that she loved Ivan perhaps more than she had ever loved anyone, her place in the Social World came first.

Edward was not only in many ways a kind and generous husband, but he was a favourite of the Prince of Wales and considered a "good chap" amongst the other Stewards of the Jockey Club and the members of White's.

To leave him would mean social ostracism from everything that made her position in life important and amusing. No-one, not even Ivan, could compensate for the loss of that.

The Prince was saying:

"Now that, as you say, I am free, I have made a big decision, and this, Odele, is where I want you to help me."

"What is your decision?"

"I must marry again!"

So he *was* thinking of marriage.

Lady Odele drew in her breath, wondering how she could refuse him without losing him.

"As you are aware," the Prince continued, "I have

no children. My wife was actually with child when the accident occurred, which left her a lunatic for the rest of her unhappy life."

For a moment his voice was hard. Then he went on:

"But now I want an heir and if possible other sons and daughters to inherit my fortune and to give me what I know will be a new interest."

Lady Odele did not speak because she found it difficult to know what she should say.

"I have thought over the idea carefully," the Prince went on, "and I realise that in my large acquaintance of friends I know very few women of the right age."

"What age is that?" Lady Odele asked, thinking her voice sounded very unlike her own.

"That is another thing I have thought over carefully," the Prince said. "I want the mother of my children to be pure and innocent of love except for what I shall teach her."

Lady Odele stared at him in astonishment.

Could Ivan really have said "pure and innocent"? It certainly seemed strange from a man who was notorious over the whole of Europe for his love-affairs.

She thought of the hundreds of beautiful women who had thrown their hearts and their bodies at his feet only too eagerly.

Then as if she realised that she must say something, she said almost tartly:

"In which case your wife will have to be very young."

"Exactly!" the Prince agreed.

"A young girl on the threshold of womanhood?"

"That is the person I have in mind."

"Are you telling me that you have already asked someone to marry you?" Lady Odele enquired.

Despite her intention to remain cool and calm, she could not restrain the note of indignation that crept

13

into her voice and the sharpness that invaded the liquid beauty of her eyes.

The Prince shook his head.

"That is the trouble," he said. "I know exactly what I want, but as you must be aware, Odele, I never meet young girls. They appear not to exist in a world which is filled with sophisticated beauties like yourself."

Lady Odele gave an almost audible sigh of relief.

Now she was beginning to understand why he had turned to her for help.

"You wish to marry an English girl?"

"As you know, I find the English as a race attractive," he said, giving her a meaningful look with something very intimate in it, "and I like the way Englishwomen who are well bred have a pride and a self-control which is hard to find in the women of other nations."

"You are also half-English."

Lady Odele knew as she spoke that he was intensely proud of his English blood and had followed his father in being completely alienated from everything that was Russian.

The late Prince Katinouski had quarrelled with the Tzar and had left St. Petersburg for Europe, never to return.

He had married the Duke of Warminster's daughter, and his only son, Prince Ivan, had been brought up in an entirely English fashion.

He had been sent to Eton and to Oxford, and it was only after this that his Russian blood and his great wealth had taken him to all the pleasure-spots of the world and people had begun to talk of Ivan Katinouski as if he were a character out of the *Arabian Nights*. and his race-horses in England were all comprised in the legend of the fairy-tale Prince.

His parties in Paris, his extravagances in Italy,

But it was inevitable that people talked most about the women he loved.

They pursued him frantically, loving him to the point where they risked their reputations in a reckless fashion if his dark eyes so much as looked in their direction.

"I suppose an English wife would suit you best," Lady Odele agreed a little doubtfully.

As she spoke, she was wondering how any English girl could cope, as even she was unable to do, with the many diverse and strange sides of the Prince's character.

Lady Odele knew, if she was honest, that while she believed that he loved her at least for the moment and that she attracted him passionately, she could not have gone into a witness-box on her oath and sworn that she knew him as a man.

There was so much that was secret about him, so many unfathomed depths to his character that even to think of them left her bewildered.

Aloud she said:

"Perhaps, Ivan, a girl of a different nationality might be more suitable."

Then as she spoke she knew that she was being foolish.

What did it matter if Ivan's wife did not understand him? She would be there only to give him what he demanded in regard to children.

She was not surprised when the Prince answered her remark by saying:

"I know what I want, Odele. I wish you to find me an English girl from, of course, a noble family, who will give me children and fill the part of my life that has been empty all these years."

As if she could not help herself, Lady Odele said with a faint smile:

"Are you really telling me, Ivan, that there has

been something missing? I always thought everything about your life was complete and perfect."

"As complete as it was possible to be," the Prince added, "but always in the background of my life has been the wife to whom I was married for only six months."

There was no need for him to say more.

Even Lady Odele's limited imagination could conjure up a picture of the poor, mad creature who bore his name, hidden away in Hungary while he wandered the world alone.

It struck her with an unusual perception, because she was not a very imaginative woman, that with all his houses, Castles, *Châteaux*, and Palaces, not one of them, without a wife and family, was really a home.

Because she knew he expected it of her, she said, speaking in a different tone from the one she had used before:

"Of course I will help you, Ivan. Tell me exactly what you want and I will do everything in my power to bring it about."

As she spoke, she thought to herself that in that way she could hold him.

Society consisted of a great number of wives who sat at home, diligent and virtuous, while their husbands went a-roaming.

If Ivan decided to marry somebody like herself, Lady Odele knew she would be wildly jealous and afraid that his wife would supplant her in his affections.

But a young girl who was asked only to bear his children would not encroach for one moment on their special relationship, any more than Edward interfered so long as she was discreet.

"I think I know what you want," she said, "someone young, very well bred, and I suppose pretty."

The Prince smiled and for the moment it swept from his face everything that was serious.

"I do not think I could tolerate looking at a plain face over the breakfast-table," he said. "Yes, Odele, she will have to be pretty, but I cannot expect or even hope for somebody as beautiful as you."

"Very well," Lady Odele said. "I will have a look round at the débutantes who came out this year. There must be one . . ."

She stopped suddenly and gave a little cry.

"But of course! I know the very girl! I cannot imagine why I did not think of her first."

"Who is she?" the Prince enquired.

"My niece, Charlotte Storr."

Before her marriage Lady Odele had been a Storr and her brother was now the Earl of Storrington.

It was impossible to query the importance or the breeding of the Storrs, who had played their parts in history since the first Storrington had held an important position at the Court of Henry VIII.

There had always been Storrs in the Army and the Navy who had been decorated for gallantry, just as there had been Storrs in the House of Lords who had played their parts as Statesmen and had been in attendance on whichever King or Queen was reigning at the moment.

Every Countess of Storrington was a hereditary Lady-of-the-Bedchamber, just as every Earl held an important post in the Royal Household.

"Why have I never heard of your niece before?" the Prince enquired.

"Charlotte should have been presented this year," Lady Odele replied, "but my sister-in-law was in mourning for her mother. Charlotte has therefore remained in the School-Room, although she is eighteen."

The Prince was listening and Lady Odele continued:

"She is a pretty child."

"Like you?"

"A little. Most of the Storrs have blue eyes and

17

fair hair. She will certainly meet your conditions of being pure and innocent."

The Prince gave a sigh of relief.

"Arrange for me to meet her," he said. "We might have another party in a fortnight's time, and you and I will compile the guest-list together."

"We will do that," Lady Odele said eagerly, "but we must not include the Prince and Mrs. Langtry."

The Prince rose to sit down beside her on the sofa.

"Now that that is settled," he said, "let us talk about ourselves."

She put her hand in his and as he felt a little tremor go through her at his touch, he smiled and turned it palm upwards towards his lips.

* * *

The Viscount handed his gun to the Keeper, saying to his companion as he did so:

"That was jolly good shooting, Shane. I have never seen a better right and left."

"I was rather pleased with it myself," the Honourable Shane O'Derry replied. "But I thought you were a bit off form today, Richard."

"The result of too much port last night," the Viscount confessed, "but after all that walking, I feel better than I did first thing this morning."

"So do I," Shane O'Derry agreed.

They thanked the Keeper and walked towards the shooting-brake which would carry them to Storrington Park.

As they sat in it bumping over the rough roads which led from the farm-land on which they had been shooting partridges back towards the main drive, they looked almost as if they might be brothers.

There was, however, no blood relationship between them, but they had been close friends ever since they had been educated at the same Public School, and they were now, after leaving the same University, intent on enjoying the gaiety and social life of London together.

This was easy for theViscount, whose father could afford to give him a handsome allowance, while Shane O'Derry seldom had two guineas to clink together in his pocket.

The second son of the Earl of Dunderry, an impoverished Irish Peer with a crumbling Castle and few meagre rents from his poverty-stricken tenants, the future of the Honourable Shane would have been bleak except for the fact that his friend Richard was prepared to share everything he owned with him.

They were in fact teasingly called "the Inseparables."

Now laughing together at some intimate joke, they ran up the steps of the house and wended their way towards their bedrooms in the West Wing, where the Viscount had a Sitting-Room that had been his special Sanctum ever since he had been a young boy.

It was shabby, untidy, and cluttered with an extraordinary mixture of sporting-trophies, tennis-racquets, cricket-bats, and everything else which found a place on the floor because there was no space left on the walls.

Occasionally the Countess ordered the House-keeper to see that the room was put in order, but the moment her back was turned it lapsed into the same tangled mess and she gave up the almost unequal task of trying to keep her son in order.

"I must say I have never enjoyed a day more," Shane said, "but I am damned thirsty."

"Ale or cider?" the Viscount asked. "I dare not ask for anything more intoxicating at this time of day, or Gilpin will undoubtedly tell my father."

"Cider is all I need," Shane replied.

The Viscount moved as if to reach for the bell-pull, then said:

"I am quite certain the bell is broken. I will go and shout down the back-stairs."

He went from the room as he spoke, and Shane moved to the window to look out over the Park with its ancient oak trees and the huge well-tended garden.

He heard somebody come into the room behind him, and, thinking it was the Viscount, he did not turn his head until a soft voice called:

"Shane!"

He turned then eagerly to see a young girl looking at him.

"Charlotte!" he murmured.

Then she ran frantically across the room to throw herself against him.

"Shane! Shane!" she cried, and he heard her voice break on his name.

"What is the matter? What has upset you?" he asked.

"I ... I cannot tell you—oh, Shane—I think my —heart will break!"

"You must tell me—what is it?"

He held her close against him and he knew as her face was hidden that she was crying.

His arms tightened and he kissed her hair, and as he did so, the Viscount came back into the room.

"I told one of the footmen to bring me ..." he began, then saw his sister in Shane's arms. "What is the matter? What has happened?"

"That is what I am trying to find out," Shane replied. "Charlotte is upset."

"Do not let Mama see you like that," the Viscount warned.

His sister raised her head from Shane's shoulder. "Mama is—in the Drawing-Room," she said almost incoherently, "and—I came to tell you—what has happened."

The tears were pouring down her pale cheeks and her blue eyes were swimming with them.

"Come and sit down," Shane suggested gently. "Tell us what has upset you."

"It is not like you to be a cry-baby, Charlotte," the Viscount remarked.

"Y-you would—cry if you were in—m-my shoes!" Charlotte retorted almost fiercely.

"Tell us what it is all about," her brother said.

Shane had taken Charlotte to a large arm-chair which stood at one side of the fireplace.

As she sat down on it, he perched on the arm.

Drawing a handkerchief from the pocket of his tweed coat, he wiped her eyes.

Because he was gentle about it, it seemed to make her want to cry all the more.

With an effort she forced away her tears and, holding tightly to his hand, said in a voice that was still very shaken:

"M-Mama has had a—letter from Aunt Odele. She has—found a—h-husband for m-me."

"A husband?" the Viscount exclaimed. "Good Heavens, you have not yet been presented!"

"I—know," Charlotte replied, "b-but Aunt Odele wrote that I was—the luckiest girl in the world—and that the whole—family should go down on their knees and thank—G-God for such a wonderful—opportunity."

"Whom has she in mind? It sounds as though it might be the Prince of Wales, except that he is married."

As the Viscount spoke, he saw that his friend Shane had gone very white and was looking at Charlotte with an expression of such pain in his eyes that it was impossible not to be aware of his suffering.

The Viscount was the only person in the house

who had the least idea that Charlotte and Shane were
in love with each other and had been for years.

To the Viscount it had seemed almost inevitable
and certainly natural that they should love each other,
especially as they were the two people for whom he
had the deepest affection.

Now for the first time he saw the tragic conse-
quences in which their love could involve them.

He supposed, if he thought about it, he would
have been aware that Charlotte would be expected to
make what his mother would call a good marriage if
not a brilliant one.

Shane, as a second son with no money at all,
would certainly not be considered an eligible suitor.

"And who does Aunt Odele suggest you should
marry?" he asked aloud.

"I—I will not do as she says!" Charlotte cried.
"N-nothing will make me marry anyone except
Shane. But Mama is already excited by the idea—
and I know Papa will be too—when she tells him
about it."

The tears were back in her eyes and running
down her cheeks.

"Oh, Shane—save me—save me!"

Because she sounded so piteous, Shane knelt
down beside the chair to hold her in his arms.

It was the Viscount who heard the footman's
rather heavy tread outside the door.

"Look out!" he said sharply in a low voice.

As Shane got hastily to his feet, Charlotte turned
her face quickly towards the fireplace so that the servant would not see her tears.

The Viscount rose to take a tray containing two
glasses and a large jug of cider from the footman.

"Thank you, James," he said, "that will be all."

He put the tray down on the table, shoving aside
a number of things that were in the way to make a
place for it, then poured out the cider.

As the door shut behind the footman, he said:

"You must be careful. If the servants report to Mama that you were crying in Shane's arms, he would be sent back to Ireland on the next boat."

"I will—try to be careful," Charlotte answered, "but if I have to marry this horrible—beastly man whom Aunt Odele has chosen for me—I swear I will kill myself."

"You are not to talk like that, darling," Shane said in a low voice.

He took Charlotte's hand in his as he spoke, and she clung to it as if it were a lifeline that would save her from drowning.

"Who is the man?" the Viscount asked.

For a moment it seemed as if Charlotte was incapable of answering.

Then at length, with her eyes on Shane, in a voice her brother could barely hear, she said:

"Prince Ivan Katinouski!"

For a moment both the Viscount and Shane seemed frozen into immobility. Then her brother managed to say:

"I do not believe it! It is impossible! It must be a joke!"

Chapter Two

"It is not a joke," Charlotte said fiercely. "Mama —read me the—letter—then somebody called to see her and I—snatched it up from her—writing-table."

As she spoke, she fumbled in her sash and drew out a letter that was rather creased. She looked down at it and said brokenly: "I—cannot see—you—read it," and held it out to her brother.

She then turned her tear-stained face towards Shane.

The Viscount took it from her and looked down at the impressive crest on the thick white paper. Then he read aloud:

"*My Dearest Margaret:*

I have the most exciting news for you which seems incredible, but I feel that when you hear what it is, you will thank God for such a wonderful opportunity for dear little Charlotte.

I am staying here with Prince Ivan Katinouski and he has told me that his wife, the Princess, who has been mad for the last twelve years, has now died. Because I am such an old friend, he has asked me to help him choose a wife.

25

As you know, he is one of the richest men in Europe, if not the world, and also he is admired and liked everywhere he goes.

He could, of course, marry anybody, but he wants someone young and unspoilt, in his own words 'pure and innocent,' who comes from a noble family and who will be not only the Chatelaine of his many magnificent houses but also the mother of the children that he has never been able to have.

I am well aware, dear Margaret, that George does not care for foreigners, but Prince Ivan is exceptional in that his mother was a Warminster, and nobody can say that the Warminsters are anything but the most English of the English!

I know that Charlotte, having been in mourning for your dear mother, has seen nothing of the world, but that is what Prince Ivan would wish, and I therefore am arranging on his behalf a house-party on the eighteenth, here at Charl, where he and Charlotte can get to know each other.

I am making it a young party as you know how zealous in pursuing him all the ambitious mother's of young girls will be, when they learn that the Prince is now eligible.

I therefore think it best for me to chaperone Charlotte and for you to send her to me with Richard and, if he wishes to come, his inseparable friend Shane O'Derry.

I know it is somewhat short notice, but I am sure you will agree that this is Charlotte's chance to make a really brilliant marriage, and it would be a mistake to have the Prince's interests diverted elsewhere.

I am so excited at the prospect of my niece living here at Charl and at all the other fantastic houses the Prince owns, and I will let you know the time she and Richard should arrive, as soon as I know myself.

I remain, dear Margaret,
        Your affectionate sister-in-law,
                Odele."

The Viscount read the letter aloud with an un-mistakable note of surprise in his voice, and as he finished he said angrily:

"It is the most impertinent, outrageous thing I have ever heard! How dare the Prince, and Aunt Odele for that matter, treat Charlotte as if she were a piece of merchandise to be bought over the counter!"

"That is naturally what I think too," Shane said in a low voice.

Charlotte made a cry like that of a small animal caught in a trap.

"It is—horrible! Wicked!" she sobbed. "But I knew—when Mama—read me the letter that she was —delighted."

"Perhaps your father ..." Shane began hesitatingly.

"There is no hope there," the Viscount interrupted. "I am sure Papa does not like the Prince as a man, but he is terribly impressed by his horses. Who would not be?"

"I will not—marry him—and—nothing will—make me!" Charlotte cried.

Her brother and Shane O'Derry did not speak. They looked at each other and they were both thinking that Charlotte would have little choice in the matter.

She was only just eighteen, so her parents could force her to marry anybody they wished and there would be no appeal against their decision.

"What can we do?" Shane asked, and his voice seemed strangled in his throat.

"It is intolerable!" the Viscount declared, throwing down the letter and getting up to walk across the room and back again.

27

"Your aunt seems to think that he might become interested in somebody else if you do not act speedily," Shane said hesitatingly. "Suppose Charlotte was ill and could not stay at Charl on the eighteenth?"

"Aunt Odele will not let her off the hook so easily," the Viscount replied bitterly. "And her behaviour is all the more surprising in this matter when you and I both know that she and the Prince—"

He stopped suddenly, as if he realised he was being indiscreet.

Charlotte raised her head from Shane's shoulder to ask:

"What about Aunt Odele and the Prince?"

"They are—old friends, she says so in the letter," her brother said hastily.

"You mean—something more than that—do you not?"

There was silence. Then Charlotte asked:

"Can their—relationship be the—same as—that of the Prince of Wales and the beautiful—Mrs. Langtry?"

She looked from her brother to Shane, then said:

"B-but Aunt Odele is quite—old!"

"Their relationship has nothing to do with your marrying the Prince," the Viscount said testily.

"It has!" Charlotte objected. "If she is—in love with him and he with her, how can I be—made to—marry him? It is wicked, as I said—really wicked!"

Nobody spoke for a moment. Then the Viscount said furiously:

"Charlotte is right, it *is* wicked! We ought to do something about it."

"What can we do," Shane asked helplessly, "except provide him with someone he might prefer to Charlotte?"

"It is not even a case of preferring. He demands someone pure, innocent, and noble. I am surprised he

28

has not asked for the goods he requires to be marked down at half-price!"

The Viscount spoke angrily as he walked to the window and opened it to draw in some fresh air.

Then with his back to Shane and Charlotte he said:

"What I would like to do is pay him back by making him look a fool, but God knows how we could ever do that."

"Perhaps Wilbram could help us," Shane said.

"Wilbram?" the Viscount asked, walking back from the window to the fireplace. "How could he help?"

Then, before Shane could answer, he said:

"I know what you are thinking of—that bet he won!"

"What—bet?" Charlotte enquired, looking helplessly at her brother.

Her eyes were still full of tears and she looked so pathetic that Shane sat down beside her in the big arm-chair to hold her even closer in his arms.

"He is a friend of ours," Shane explained, "and he was so annoyed with the Marchioness of Troon, who he said was a snob, that he got a woman invited to one of her parties and passed her off as the Grand Duchess of Melkinstein, or some such place, whereas in reality she was nothing but..."

The Viscount coughed warningly and Shane changed what he had been about to say to "a ballet-dancer."

"And everybody was taken in?" Charlotte asked.

"They were," the Viscount said, "but of course Wilbram and his friends dressed her to look the part."

Charlotte looked appealingly at her brother.

"Could we not do—something like that?"

"We would never get away with it," the Viscount answered. "There is no-one with more experience of women than the Prince."

"We could if we found the right girl for the part," Shane suggested, "and the Prince liked her more than Charlotte."

"I could make myself look ugly," Charlotte said eagerly, "and be rude and disagreeable so that he would tell Aunt Odele he had no wish to marry me."

Again the two men's eyes met.

"I am sure Aunt Odele has thought this up and the Prince will marry whomever she chooses," the Viscount said after a moment.

"But we could—try," Charlotte said desperately, "please—let us—try."

The Viscount was watching his sister and he thought for the first time in his life that arranged marriages were sheer, undiluted cruelty.

He had never thought of it before, taking it as a matter of course that noble families should marry into noble families because it was in their best interests.

But he had never thought that anyone as inexperienced and childish as Charlotte could be married to somebody as sophisticated as the Prince, and he knew that for her, marriage, especially as she was in love with Shane, would be a misery beyond words.

As a sportsman he admired the Prince, as did all his friends, and they followed his prowess on the Turf with the greatest interest.

He had of course, from time to time, met him casually at parties and had seen him in White's Club, to which he had recently been elected a member.

But although the Prince moved in a very much higher stratum of society than anything he and Shane aspired to, he was well aware of the gossip about the handsome Russian.

In fact, he had not been particularly surprised when he learnt that his latest *inamorata* was none other than his Aunt Odele.

The Storrs as a family did not approve of Lady

Odele, her publicity horrified them, and they thought it very vulgar that photographs of her could be bought in the stationery-shops.

Yet, despite the fact that they had a great many criticisms to make privately about her behaviour, as long as Lady Odele was *persona grata* at Marlborough House, and both the Prince of Wales and the Princess admitted her to their friendship, there was really nothing they could do about it.

But what his aunt did, the Viscount thought, was a very different thing from involving his sister with a man who he was quite certain would make an extremely unsuitable husband and with whom she would be desperately unhappy.

Besides, he had always believed that somehow, eventually Charlotte would marry Shane, and they would all three continue to be happy together as they had been ever since they were children.

Every instinct in the Viscount's mind told him that he must do something to save his sister. The difficulty was what it could be.

"If Wilbram got away with it, I do not see why we should not," Shane was saying, not very optimistically.

"Wilbram only had to find a woman to act a part for Troon for one evening," the Viscount replied, "and a party at Troon House is rather different from one at Charl."

As if he refused to accept defeat, Shane said to Charlotte:

"Think of your friends, dearest. What about that pretty girl who stayed here a fortnight ago?"

"Alice Bracknell?" Charlotte asked. "But she is so stupid! I do not believe any man would be interested in her for more than five minutes. Besides, her mother has already determined that she shall marry Lord Dare."

"That reminds me," the Viscount said, "when I

31

was in Church about a month ago I saw the prettiest girl I have ever seen in my life. I meant to ask you who she was, but it slipped my mind."

"What were you doing in Church?" Shane queried.

"It was when you were in Ireland," the Viscount explained, "and it was my father and mother's twenty-fifth Wedding-Anniversary."

"Then of course you had to go," Shane replied. "What about this girl?"

"I know who you mean!" Charlotte said. "It was Alana. She is very pretty."

"She had a mass of children with her," the Viscount said.

"They are the Vicar's children. Alana is helping Mrs. Bredon to look after them."

"Is she really lovely?" Shane asked.

"I thought her absolutely beautiful!" the Viscount replied. "She took my mind off the Vicar's sermon, which went on for far too long, so that Papa was fidgeting about and pulling out his watch long before the end."

"We were talking about a girl," Shane persisted, as if he wanted to keep to the point.

"You are not suggesting . . ." the Viscount began.

"Why not?" Shane asked. "I would suggest anything—snatch at any straw if it would save Charlotte."

"I want to—marry you, Shane," Charlotte said. "You promised we would be married eventually—even if we—had to—wait."

"I know, dearest," Shane said, "but if I went to your father now, I hardly think he would listen to me."

"You need not waste your breath," the Viscount interposed. "Papa may not like Prince Ivan, because he hates all foreigners, but if Mama and Aunt Odele think it a good marriage, anything he has to say on the matter will be swept to one side, and Charlotte will be pushed up the aisle as quickly as her feet can carry her!"

Charlotte put her hand up to her eyes and started to cry again.

"Dammit, we have to do something!" he added. "Do you suppose we could get this girl to help us? Bribe her into taking the Prince's attention away from Charlotte?"

His sister had stopped crying and was looking at him with widening eyes.

"Are you really suggesting that we might take— Alana with us to—Charl?"

"Not as herself," the Viscount said. "Supposing we pretended that she was someone smart and noble. That would please the Prince, and it might take his mind off you at least for a little while."

"The only alternative," Shane said, "would be for us to run away now, at once."

"Papa would come after you."

"He might not find us, and then what could he do about it?"

There was silence while the Viscount looked at his friend and saw the expression of despair in his eyes.

"If only this had not happened so quickly," Charlotte said. "You know when I am twenty-one I come into the money my Godmother left me."

"I had forgotten that," her brother replied. "How much is it?"

"I think it is only about two hundred or three hundred pounds a year, but Papa said something about it accumulating and that it would be more by the time I came of age."

"We have discussed this," Shane said apologetically, "and I know my father would give us a house on the Estate. I could breed horses or something. We would be able to manage."

"Of course we would!" Charlotte agreed. "And we would be so happy, so very, very happy."

She looked up into Shane's eyes as she spoke, and for a moment they forgot everything but themselves.

"There is no chance of your waiting until Charlotte is twenty-one," the Viscount said sharply. "It is a question of acting now, if we are to get her away from the Prince."

Charlotte looked at her brother and asked:

"Are you really—thinking of—Alana?"

"Tell me about her. She is certainly very pretty."

"She is lovely and very sweet."

"How do you know her?"

"She was Mr. Wickham's daughter."

"Wickham?"

"My music-teacher. You must have met him. He came here three times a week for years."

"Of course, I remember now. A tall, rather good-looking man."

"I always thought him very handsome," Charlotte said, "and absolutely charming. Of course Mama treated him as she treated all my teachers, as if he were dirt beneath her feet, but actually he was a gentleman, although she would not have thought so."

"How do you know?" the Viscount asked.

"He told me once that his family were well known in the North, and his father had been a famous Conductor."

Her brother gave a short laugh.

"Mama would not think that qualified him as a gentleman."

"I know," Charlotte agreed, "but he was, and I loved my music-lessons with him, although I shall never be able to play as well as he or Alana."

"So that is how you met her."

"She came here first because Mr. Wickham and I played duets together on our violins and Alana accompanied us on the piano. She could play the violin too. I would have liked to have her as a friend, but of course Mama would not have heard of such a thing."

"Of course not!" her brother agreed. "But you still see her?"

"Only in Church now. When her father died, the servants told me she had been left with no money. Then, while I was plucking up the courage to ask Mama if I could be kind to her, I heard that she had moved to the Vicarage to help Mrs. Bredon with all those children."

"I should think that would be a dog's life," the Viscount remarked.

"Mrs. Bredon is kind, but there are five children."

"I should think that in the circumstances," Shane said, "she would be delighted to get away from them for a bit and stay at somewhere like Charl."

"Do you really mean that?" Charlotte asked.

The Viscount was thinking.

"I cannot believe we would find a prettier girl if we searched the whole County, and if, as Charlotte says, her father was a gentleman, she will know how to behave."

Charlotte looked from one to the other.

"Oh, Richard, this is a wonderful idea! If I ask Alana to come for my sake, I am sure she would. I think she was really fond of me and actually I have missed seeing her since her father died."

The Viscount looked at his friend.

"Shall we give it a try, Shane? It really would be a jest if we could pull the Prince's leg and deceive him into being fooled by a girl who is nothing but a mother's-helper at the Vicarage."

"I think it depends on whether she is as attractive as you say she is," Shane said, "and also if she can act the part of a grand lady."

"We also have to get her into Charl somehow. We can hardly appear and tell the Prince we have brought the Queen of Sheba with us because she thought she would like to see his house."

"I could say she was staying with me," Charlotte suggested. "As neither Mama or Papa is coming with me, there is no reason for Aunt Odele to be suspicious. She does not know any of my friends."

"We might get away with it," the Viscount said doubtfully, then he gave a cry.

"I have it! I have a splendid idea!"

"What is it?" Charlotte asked breathlessly.

"If you can get this girl to agree to come with us, we will say that she is Shane's sister, Lady Alana O'Derry!"

"My sister?" Shane exclaimed. "I have two of them, but the eldest is only fifteen."

"How is the Prince to know that?"

"Aunt Odele might know," Charlotte said.

"As a matter of fact, there are lots of O'Derrys in Ireland," Shane replied. "I think it would be better if she were my cousin. Papa's brother, from whom he inherited the title, had several daughters."

"Then she is your first cousin," the Viscount agreed. "She has arrived unexpectedly from Ireland to stay with us, and so we could do nothing but bring her with us to Charl. Does that sound plausible?"

"It sounds perfect!" Charlotte cried. "But I have to get Alana to agree."

"We could pay her to come. I am sure she could do with twenty pounds, or more if she insists."

"I have a feeling," Charlotte replied, "that to offer her money would be a mistake. Mr. Wickham was very proud and I am sure Alana is too. I think it would be better if I told her the truth and asked her to help me."

"Do you think she would do that?"

"I hope she would. She is very idealistic, and I am sure she would be shocked at my being pushed

into marriage with a man I have never even seen—
especially as I love Shane."

"Well, you persuade her any way you like," the
Viscount said, "as long as she agrees."

"I can only try my best."

"We will tell Mama we are going driving tomorrow morning. We will leave you at the Vicarage
and pick you up again about an hour later."

"That is a good idea," Charlotte replied. "I might
have seen Alana in that way before now if I had
thought of it, but you know what Mama has always
been like about our mixing with anyone in the village."

They all knew that this was true.

The Earl and Countess of Storrington kept themselves very much apart from what they called "the
locals."

Once a year, the Vicar and Mrs. Bredon were
invited to dinner with the Doctor and his wife and
one or two other people who lived on the Earl's vast
Estates but were not considered important enough
to be on intimate terms with those who lived in the
big house.

Their real friends included all the important
County families who lived within driving distance
and those who came from London for several weeks'
rest in the country during the summer, or for shooting, hunting, and Balls in the winter.

Charlotte had not been allowed to take part in
such activities, being still in the School-Room, but it
did not worry her because when Richard was at
home, Shane was nearly always with him and she
had no wish to see anyone else.

The Earl and Countess had three younger children, all boys, who were at the moment at Boarding-
Schools.

As if he felt now they had made a decision and

the tension of Charlotte's news was for the moment somewhat relaxed, the Viscount picked up the letter from their aunt, which he had flung on the floor, and handed it back to his sister.

"If you take my advice," he said, "you will wash your face and try to look a bit more cheerful. It is no use letting Mama get the idea that you intend to oppose this marriage. It might make her put Aunt Odele on her guard. We must all behave quite naturally until we find out if Alana What's-her-name will help you."

"That is very sensible," Shane agreed.

He pulled Charlotte a little closer to him as he said:

"You had better do as Richard says and try not to be unhappy, dearest. We will save you somehow, if not in this way, then we will find another."

"Do you mean that—do you really—mean it?" Charlotte asked.

"Prince or no Prince, I am not going to let you marry him or any other man, that I swear!"

There was a possessive note in Shane's voice which brought a light to Charlotte's eyes and a smile to her lips as she said:

"Darling—I have been so—frightened."

"Trust Richard and me."

"I do!"

She kissed Shane's cheek as she rose from the chair, then took the letter from her brother's hand.

"Thank you, Richard—thank you—thank you!" she said. "You are the most wonderful brother in the world!"

Without waiting for him to reply, she went from the room.

Shane got to his feet.

"Do you think we have a chance?" he asked in a low voice.

"We can only hope and pray," the Viscount replied. "You know what the Prince is like. Charlotte could never cope with a man like him."

"The whole idea makes me want to kill him!" Shane said fiercely. "I swear to you, that is what I will do rather than let Charlotte marry him."

"Hold on!" the Viscount said. "I know what your Irish temper is like. I cannot have Charlotte a widow before she is even married!"

"I bet you this is entirely your aunt's idea."

"Of course it is! She is madly in love with the man, just as all his other women are, and she thinks that if he has a nice, innocent girl like Charlotte as his wife, she will not be aware of what is going on behind her back."

"The whole thing makes me sick!" Shane said. "I promise you this, Richard, if we cannot save Charlotte by making a fool of the Prince, then I will either kill him or take her away to Ireland and hide her where nobody will find her."

"You cannot marry her without Papa's permission while she is under eighteen."

"I will marry her somehow," Shane said confidently. "You know as well as I do, Richard, that I cannot lose her."

"No, I know that," the Viscount agreed, "but it is not going to be easy."

"That is not important," Shane answered. "What we are doing is morally right, and I believe in all sincerity that because of that, we will defeat the evil plans of your aunt and the damned Prince."

"I hope so," the Viscount agreed.

But there was a note of doubt in the words as he said them.

*　　*　　*

Alana picked up the youngest Bredon child, who was only three and who was crying because his five-year-old sister had taken his ball away from him.

"Never mind," she said in a soft, musical voice. "I will find you something else to play with."

"Ball! Ball!" he sobbed.

She sat him down on her knee, holding him closely and rocking him against her breast until his tears abated.

"That is better," she said with a smile, "and now I will find you another ball."

She looked round as she spoke and saw a small skein of brightly coloured wool with which she had been mending one of the other children's socks.

Carrying little Billy in her arms, she took the wool from the chest-of-drawers and, still holding him, wound it round her fingers into some semblance of a ball.

He watched her, fascinated, then clenched it tightly in his small, fat hands.

"Ball! Ball!" he cried, and now he was laughing.

Alana wiped his cheeks with her handkerchief, kissed him, and set him down on the floor.

"Go play with your ball," she ordered, "while I tidy the room."

As she spoke, she went to the window to look out and see that the other four children, whom she had sent to play in the Vicarage-garden, were all right.

She had wrapped them up warmly in their thick coats and woollen caps, but she saw that one of the girls had already lost her cap, and the eldest boy, who was ten, was throwing his up into a tree, trying to get it caught on one of the branches.

She told herself that although it might be difficult to get it down again, it would not be impossible, and at least he was not throwing stones at the others, which yesterday had ended with two cracked windows.

"I have tidied the room," she said to Billy, who

was now sitting happily on the floor playing with his woollen ball. "Now I will put on your warm clothes and we will all go for a long walk."

She knew of old that exercise was the best way of curbing the exuberance of the older children, and she was thinking that as Billy was getting too heavy for her to carry very far, she would have to take him in his push-cart.

The door opened but she did not glance round, thinking it was either Mrs. Bredon or the daily woman who came in to do the rough work but often left the place rougher than it was when she had started.

"Hello, Alana!" a soft voice said.

Alana started.

"Lady Charlotte!" she exclaimed. "I was not expecting to see you!"

"I saw a funny old woman on the doorstep who told me you were in the Nursery."

"That is Mrs. Hicks," Alana explained. "She is a bit mad and she might easily have sent you to the cellar or the attic!"

Charlotte laughed.

"Alana, you always say such amusing things. I have missed you so much."

"As I have missed you."

"You know I would have come to see you if I could."

"Yes, I know that."

Charlotte looked round the cluttered room.

"Are you all right here?" she asked.

"The Vicar and Mrs. Bredon have been very kind," Alana replied. "After Papa died, I found I had no money . . . and quite a lot of . . . debts."

"Oh, poor Alana! I felt terrible that I could not help you. You must forgive me."

"There is nothing to forgive, Lady Charlotte. Why should you help me?"

41

"Because we were friends," Charlotte answered, "but I have proved a very bad one, and I am ashamed of myself."

Alana laughed and it was a very pretty sound.

"Now you are being ridiculous, but it is lovely to see you. Will you not sit down?"

As she spoke, she went to the window to see if the children were all right, and to her relief they had taken their rabbits out of the hutch and were playing with them on the grass.

They were very large, fat, lazy rabbits that had no wish to run away, and Alana thought she need not trouble about the children at least for a short time.

"I have come to see you, Alana," Charlotte was saying, "because I—need your help. It may sound a very—selfish reason—but I am—desperate."

"Desperate?" Alana questioned.

She sat down opposite Charlotte, who bent forward to say in a low voice:

"You know, because I told you, that I love Shane O'Derry and that I have always intended to marry him?"

"Yes, you told me that a long time ago," Alana replied. "What has happened? He has not . . . ?"

"No, no! It is nothing Shane has done," Charlotte said hastily. "It is just that today I have had a terrible shock!"

Quickly she told Alana exactly what had happened, but she could not help her voice breaking on the words and the tears coming into her eyes.

"Oh, Lady Charlotte, I am so sorry!" Alana cried. "I do understand what you are going through. Of course your father and mother have no idea that you are in love with somebody else. Could you not tell them?"

"They would not listen if I did," Charlotte replied. "They would merely send Shane away and I would never see him again."

"They should be thinking of your happiness."

"You say that because your father was so different from mine," Charlotte said. "I think he was the kindest man I have met in my life."

"He was kind," Alana agreed. "He often said to me: 'I hope, my darling, that one day you will fall deeply in love in the same way as I loved your mother, more and more every day until she died.'"

"I hope you will too," Charlotte said.

"It is unlikely," Alana replied, "because I shall never marry."

"Never marry!" Charlotte exclaimed. "Why not?"

"We were talking about you," Alana said quickly. "What do you intend to do about Prince Ivan?"

"That is what I have come to tell you."

Alana looked puzzled, but she did not interrupt as Charlotte went on:

"Richard and Shane were talking about some friend of theirs who took a ballet-dancer to a party in London and passed her off as a Grand Duchess. They wanted to teach their hostess a lesson because they believed her to be a snob."

Alana did not speak, but her large eyes were fixed on Charlotte's face as she continued:

"Nobody guessed that the girl was a fake, and when Richard said he had seen you in Church and how beautiful you were . . ."

Charlotte's voice faltered. Then she said:

"This seems a—preposterous thing to ask you—but, Alana, if you—say 'no'—I will be—forced to marry this—horrible—beastly man who is—in love with—my aunt."

"In love with your aunt!" Alana exclaimed.

"Yes—she is a great beauty. Lady Odele Ashford. You may have heard people talk about her."

"But of course!"

She smiled before she added:

"You know, people in the village talk of very

43

little except the Storrs and what goes on at the Castle."

"I am sure they find plenty to say," Charlotte said, then went on:

"What Richard and Shane have suggested is that if you would come with us to—Charl Castle to stay with the Prince—pretending to be Shane's cousin—then, because you are so pretty, he might take no notice of me—and in fact not ask me to be—his wife."

Alana did not move. She merely sat staring at Charlotte, who said with a little cry:

"Oh, Alana—I know it is an—impossible thing to ask of you—but what else can I do? I must marry Shane—I must! I know if Mama, Papa, and Aunt Odele all combine to force me into marriage with the Prince—they will not listen to anything I have to say —or allow me to refuse."

There was silence, then Alana asked:

"Do you really think I could ... deceive the ... Prince?"

"You simply have to look as lovely as you do now," Charlotte said, "and pretend that you are Shane's cousin. You will be—Lady Alana O'Derry—and when we arrive at the Castle—why should anybody think for a moment that you are not who we say you are?"

"I am sure the Prince, and certainly your aunt, will know at ... once that I am not ... at all grand," Alana said.

"You are supposed to be Irish," Charlotte said. "I have seen some of Shane's relatives who look like old washer-women and their clothes are terrible! But you need not worry about that—you can wear some of mine!"

Alana's eyes seemed to widen but she did not speak.

"Please—please—say you will help me," Charlotte pleaded. "You are my only—chance of escape, and I swear I am not—exaggerating when I say I would rather—die than marry anyone but Shane!"

Alana rose to her feet to walk to the window.

Now she did not look to see what the Vicar's children were doing. Instead, she stared over the trees that were losing their leaves towards the sky as if she searched in some far-off horizon for her answer.

Behind her, Charlotte, with her fingers linked together, stared at her back apprehensively.

She had a feeling that her hope for the future rested on Alana's reply.

Although she wanted to go on pleading, although she felt that there was so much more she could say, she was somehow aware that it was not words that counted at this moment but Alana's own personal feelings.

As she stood there, the pale autumn sun seemed to bring out strange, almost silver lights in her dark hair.

It was a different colour from any other hair Charlotte had ever seen before; not really dark, but more the colour of a shadow, and yet there could be strange lights in it, just as there were always, Charlotte thought, strange lights in Alana's eyes.

They were very large eyes and when she opened them wide they seemed to fill her whole face.

Sometimes when she was unhappy they looked almost purple in colour, but always there was something mysterious about them with a depth which was not to be found in other people's eyes.

'Richard is right,' Charlotte thought, 'she is perfectly lovely and she does not look like anyone else. Surely—surely the Prince will find her more attractive than me?'

Alana looked out the window for a long time. Then as Charlotte held her breath she turned to say:

"Do you really think I can help you in this, Lady

Charlotte? Because I know it would be wicked for me to say 'no,' even though I am . . . afraid of what you are . . . suggesting."

"You will do it! Oh, Alana, you will do it?"

Alana nodded.

"Yes, if you are absolutely certain that what you are doing is right."

"I am absolutely certain!" Charlotte replied in a voice that was very solemn. "It is right and good for me to marry Shane, who loves me and whom I love, and it would be wrong and wicked for me to marry Prince Ivan."

Alana gave a little sigh.

"Then I will do what you want me to do, Lady Charlotte, but you will have to help me so that I will not make mistakes and spoil everything for you."

"I know you would never do that," Charlotte said quickly, "but, oh, Alana, how can I thank you?"

As she spoke, she moved towards her and kissed her cheek.

"I am so grateful—so very, very grateful," she said, "and I know Shane will thank you from the bottom of his heart when he hears how kind you are."

Alana gave a wry little smile.

"I have told you that I shall be frightened," she said, "and that is an understatement. I should be frightened to stay at Storrington Park, let alone anywhere as famous as Charl Castle."

"You have heard of it?" Charlotte asked in surprise.

"I have read about it in the newspapers," Alana replied. "When Prince Ivan bought it, there was an article in the *Illustrated London News* and a sketch of the Castle."

"Then you know more than I do," Charlotte said. "I have only heard Richard and Shane talking about it, and of course Papa and Mama."

"Well, we shall both see it for the first time,"

Alana said. "I only hope I am not exposed as an imposter from the very moment I cross the threshold."

"Richard will see that that does not happen," Charlotte replied. "You know how clever he is at organising things. He has been the same since he was a little boy. It was always he who organised the paper-chases and musical-chairs which we played when we were children."

She smiled and went on:

"Now he organises the point-to-point meetings and steeple-chases for his friends, and the shooting-parties when Papa is too busy. Everyone says he is brilliant."

"I very much hope he will organise me," Alana said, "for I shall need to know what to say and what to do, and of course, Lady Charlotte, what to wear."

"I have told you that you can wear my clothes," Charlotte said, "and before we leave I will bring you a gown in which you can arrive and a warm travelling-cloak. As you are supposed to have just arrived from Ireland, we could say your own clothes have been lost on the journey and you are borrowing from me until yours turn up."

Alana laughed.

"I can see you are as good as your brother at make-believe."

"That is the right word," Charlotte said. "We will make it into a story like those your father used to tell me when he first started to teach me. I had always thought music was rather boring until it made it almost magic."

"That is exactly the right word," Alana said, "and now that I am without him, I miss his magic more every day."

"I think you have the same magic," Charlotte said impulsively. "That is why it was always so exciting for me to be with you both and to play in my very amateurish way with two such gifted musicians."

47

For a moment Alana's large eyes filled with tears.

"It makes me very happy to hear you say things like that. Only somebody who knew Papa as well as you did and for so many years could know how different he was from anybody else."

"I shall never forget him," Charlotte said, "and of one thing I am quite sure—if he knew what you are going to do, he would think it a huge joke!"

"I believe he would!" Alana said slowly. "And now, Lady Charlotte, you are making me feel that I cannot fail either you or Papa."

"That means," Charlotte replied, "that you have to entice the Prince away from me, and I am sure with your magic it is something you will easily be able to do!"

Chapter Three

"We have done it!" Charlotte cried as the private train started off from a side-platform at Brilling, which was the nearest station to Storrington Castle.

"So far, so good!" her brother said quietly.

His eyes were on Alana, and as she sat opposite him in one of the comfortable arm-chairs with which the Drawing-Room carriage was furnished, he was thinking that that she was even lovelier than he remembered.

This was not surprising, because Alana, in one of Charlotte's travelling-gowns, looked very different from the way she had in Church, wearing a dress she had made herself and a cheap little bonnet trimmed only with ribbons.

As Charlotte had said, Richard was a good organiser and had arranged everything they did down to the last detail.

"We must take no chances," he had said over and over again to Shane and to his sister.

Charlotte had been only too willing to agree, knowing that her whole future depended on what became a wilder and more fantastic scheme with every day that passed.

Now with Alana wearing a blue travelling-gown which was matched by the feathers in her small bonnet, and with a fur-lined cape falling from her shoulders, it was impossible to think that anyone would be suspicious that she was not what she appeared to be.

Alana herself had felt, after Charlotte had left her on the day she came to the Vicarage, that she must have dreamt everything that had been suggested.

How could she, knowing nothing of the world and having lived for so many years in a small cottage in the village, possibly act the part of a Society débutante well enough to deceive not only the Prince but also Lady Odele?

When she had told Charlotte that she had heard of her aunt, she knew that she could never repeat the stories that were circulated about the Professional Beauty by the people in the village who had known her since she was a baby.

Naturally they were extremely interested in every Storr, feeling, because they lived on the Earl's land and in the Earl's cottages, that they too were part of the family and entitled to praise or criticise them as they wished.

Lady Odele's birth, her christening, her girlhood, and her wedding to wealthy racehorse owner Sir Edward Ashford were all talked about and reminisced over by those who could remember them happening and those who wished they were old enough to remember.

But whatever age the villagers were, they were all aware that Lady Odele was a member of the Prince of Wales's smart and rather raffish set of friends.

Also Alana found, they knew the names of her

admirers almost, she thought sometimes, before Lady Odele was aware of them herself.

This was not surprising, not only as the parents of Lady Odele's lady's-maid lived in the village, but as a number of other servants in Sir Edward's employment had been trained at Storrington Park.

That Lady Odele had now captivated Prince Ivan Katinouski had been talked about for several months.

Although Alana tried not to gossip, knowing it would have shocked her father, it was impossible to be aloof or snooty in the small shops where she collected the food for the Vicarage, or to the farmer's wife from whom they bought eggs, or to anyone else who popped into the Vicarage for a chat.

She was really not surprised when Charlotte told her that they would be travelling to Charl Castle in the Prince's private train.

"Aunt Odele has written to Richard," she said, "to tell him that it will not only be more comfortable but will save the trouble of finding me a Chaperone when we cross London."

Alana waited wide-eyed as Charlotte went on:

"Of course, it is a whole lot of nonsense, and I asked Richard why I should have to be chaperoned when I am with him. But he says it is really because Aunt Odele is making very sure that there is no-one in the party to distract the Prince's attention from me!"

There was a little pause, then Charlotte said:

"Oh, Alana—Alana—you must somehow arouse his interest! Supposing after all the trouble we have taken I—have to—marry him?"

"You are making me very nervous," Alana protested. "How can I possibly interest a man like the Prince?"

"Why should you not?" Charlotte asked. "You are a thousand times prettier than I am, you are much cleverer, and you have your father's magic, which I shall never have in a thousand years!"

Alana laughed.

"You make Papa's magic sound as if it were something tangible we can hold in our hands, and which will draw the Prince like a magnet."

"That is exactly what it is," Charlotte said, "and what you must believe so that you can help me escape him."

When Charlotte had left the Vicarage, having brought a message to the Vicar to give her an excuse for seeing Alana, the latter had stood for a long time at the window looking up at the sky.

She was asking, as she had done before, for guidance, and it seemed to her almost as if her father heard the question she asked him and told her she was doing what was right.

She knew that he, of all people, would have been shocked and horrified at Charlotte being forced into marriage with any man, but most of all with the Prince.

Alana had not been speaking lightly when she told Charlotte that she had heard and read about Charl Castle and its owner.

She had also been unable to avoid listening to a great deal of scandal which percolated into the village as soon as it was known that the Prince was Lady Odele's latest admirer.

His extravagances, his numerous love-affairs, and his almost Royal way of living lost nothing in the telling.

Now as she thought of it, Alana was sure that the Viscount's plan for her to divert His Highness's attention from Charlotte to herself was as ridiculous as asking her to perform a miracle.

Nevertheless, because she loved Charlotte and for another reason which was hidden deep in the back of her mind, she had agreed to act in this charade and could only pray that she proved competent enough to deceive not only the Prince but also Lady Odele.

On Charlotte's second visit to the Vicarage, Alana had expressed a very practical fear.

"If I am successful in diverting the Prince's attention from you," she asked, "what will happen to me when he discovers that I have deceived him?"

Her large eyes were dark and wide as she spoke, but she did not add that she had lain awake for several nights worrying about this very thing.

"Richard has thought of that," Charlotte replied almost triumphantly. "He is well aware that if it is discovered who you really are, Papa might force the Vicar to dismiss you. That is why he says that as soon as the party is over you must disappear."

"Disappear?" Alana repeated faintly.

"We will have the laugh on the Prince, because he will no longer want to marry me, but we cannot do as we originally planned and tell him that you are not well born and not Shane's cousin. Instead, we are just going to say that you have gone away and we have no idea where you have gone."

"Supposing he ... insists on trying to ... find me?" Alana asked.

"I asked Richard that very question," Charlotte answered, "and he said that knowing the Prince, if he loses one woman there are hundreds of others only too willing to take her place."

"Yes ... yes, of course," Alana said quickly.

She thought that perhaps she had been presumptuous in thinking that the Prince would have any interest in her except for the few days they were at Charl.

At the same time, some practical part of her mind told her that once she disappeared, he might renew his pursuit of Charlotte.

Of course there was always the possibility that he would not find her attractive or interesting in the first place, and then all their endeavours would have been for nothing.

It was all too complicated and there were so many possibilities that they were difficult to put into words until they had actually reached Charl and seen the Prince for themselves.

"Leave everything to Richard," Charlotte kept saying, "and if all else fails, Shane and I will run away together."

She gave a little sigh as she added:

"If only we had just a little money—but Shane is always broke and it would be difficult to hide even in the wilds of Ireland, although it is very cheap, unless we had enough to keep a roof over our heads and provide us with food."

To Alana everything seemed more complicated at every turn, but because Charlotte was so insistent and because she could not bear to see her unhappy, she found herself meekly agreeing to everything that was asked of her.

She could only pray that somehow, in some magical way, everything would come right.

It was the Viscount who had thought out her excuse for leaving the Vicarage and arranged for her departure.

"You cannot say you are going away with me," Charlotte had said when she had brought Richard's instructions, "because someone is certain to mention it to Mama, and she would be astounded that you should be included in a house-party at Charl."

"Yes, of course," Alana said.

"What Richard wants you to say is that a relation you have not seen for years is passing through Brilling and will pick you up there and take you to stay with her and another relative for a few days.

You can tell Mrs. Bredon what a nuisance it is but that you feel you have to go."

"I am sure she will agree," Alana answered. "She is always very kind and understanding."

"That is what I thought," Charlotte said. "And as the Vicar will obviously not have time to drive you to Brilling, you must say that you mentioned it to me when I called today and I have said that as it happens I shall be going into the town that very day and will give you a lift."

"I hope she will not think it strange."

"Why should she," Charlotte asked, "if you say that otherwise you will have to rely on the carrier?"

"He is very unreliable," Alana ruminated, "so Mrs. Bredon will understand that I would rather accept your invitation."

"I am afraid the village will be aware that Richard and I are going to Charl Castle," Charlotte said.

"They know it already!" Alana answered. "The footmen could not wait; they came and told their parents you had been invited almost as soon as your aunt's letter arrived."

"It is frightening how everything is known."

"Everything," Alana agreed, "and therefore I am sure it is better to be quite open with the fact that you are giving me a lift to Brilling. If you picked me up in the road, somebody would be sure to see us."

"Richard always says that if one has to tell a lie, it must be a plausible one."

"The Vicar would not approve of that sentiment," Alana said with a smile, "but, at the same time, I am sure His Lordship is right."

"Just say to everybody how lucky you are to be driving into Brilling with me," Charlotte admonished, "and how much more comfortable it will be than getting there any other way."

When Charlotte had called at the Vicarage two

days before they left for Charl, Mrs. Bredon was in the Hall when she came downstairs from the Nursery.

"I hear you are going to stay at Charl Castle, Lady Charlotte," she said, making the introduction to the subject easier than Charlotte had anticipated.

"Yes, is it not exciting?" Charlotte replied. "I believe it is very magnificent, and my aunt has described it in glowing terms."

"One of the finest Castles in England, I have always heard," Mrs. Bredon said.

"I shall be able to tell you if that is true when I come back," Charlotte answered. "And I hear that Alana is going away on the same day."

"To see an elderly relative."

"I do not know how you will manage without her."

"We will manage," Mrs. Bredon replied, "but I only hope she will not be away for long."

"I have told her that I can give her a lift as far as Brilling, which will save the Vicar having to take her there," Charlotte said. "We actually pass the Vicarage door on the way to the station."

"That is indeed thoughtful of you, Lady Charlotte. In fact my husband was wondering only this morning how he would fit in such a long journey when there are so many other things to be done."

"It will be no trouble," Charlotte said. "But Alana must be ready at ten o'clock."

"I will see that she is," Mrs. Bredon promised, "and thank you very much, Lady Charlotte, for your thoughtfulness."

"I am so glad that I can be of some help, but please do not say anything about it to Mama. She does not like me to do things on my own initiative, and she might think that I was interfering."

The way Charlotte spoke made it easy for the Vicar's wife, who disliked the Countess, to understand why Lady Charlotte had not visited Alana immediately after her father's death.

In fact, the whole village had considered it rather heartless, considering how many years Mr. Wickham had journeyed up to the big house three times a week for Lady Charlotte's music-lessons.

Now Mrs. Bredon understood that Lady Charlotte, who she had always thought was a sweet young lady, was making up for her previous neglect.

"I understand, Lady Charlotte," she said soothingly, "and I shall say nothing. There is far too much chit-chat in Brilling as it is."

Alana had been picked up by the carriage and they had all four travelled to Brilling Station. There, Charlotte and Alana rushed into the Ladies' Waiting-Room with Richard's instructions that they must take no more than ten minutes.

In exactly ten minutes Alana Wickham in her cheap wool travelling-cloak and unfashionable bonnet had vanished.

In her place was the extremely elegant Lady Alana O'Derry, dressed in the very height of fashion and looking as smart as her friend, Lady Charlotte Storr.

With his usual foresight, the Viscount had sent away the Storr footman who should have waited to see them off on the train and made sure that their luggage was safely aboard.

"There is no need for you to wait, James," the Viscount had said in a lofty fashion. "As we are going in a private train, it may be delayed, and you know His Lordship does not like the horses to be kept standing about."

"Ye're quite sure ye can manage, M'Lord?" James had asked.

"You have found us a porter," the Viscount replied, "and there is really nothing else to do, so— good-bye, James."

"Good-bye, M'Lord, and Oi hopes ye have a pleasant journey," James answered.

As soon as Charlotte and Alana appeared, the Viscount hurried them quickly to the side-platform where the Prince's train was waiting.

Shane was already there, having seen to the disposal of the enormous amount of trunks Charlotte had with her.

"I have brought with me almost everything I possess," she told Alana, "so you will have a large choice for what will suit you best. Fortunately, I had a number of gowns made for the summer when I should have been presented, which Mama had forgotten about, so she has been buying me new ones ever since Aunt Odele's first letter arrived."

Alana had only a quick glimpse of her reflection in the small mirror in the cloak-room of the Ladies' Waiting-Room, but she knew she looked very unlike her usual self.

Now in the private train she felt it really must all be a dream and she would wake up to hear one of the Bredon children crying.

She had of course seen the Viscount in Church when he had first noticed her, and riding in the Park, and many times in the past when he had driven through the village or she had seen him in the distance.

But she had never spoken to him and now she thought he was an extremely good-looking, well-dressed young man and just the sort of brother Charlotte should have.

"It is very kind of you to do this for us," he said in a low voice.

"I'm only afraid that I may ... fail you," Alana answered.

On the other side of the carriage, Charlotte and Shane were looking into each other's eyes and talking in a low, intimate manner which displayed all too clearly their absorption in each other.

The Viscount gave them a quick glance and said:

"Careful how you behave! You know as well as I do that servants have ears!"

"We will be very, very careful," Charlotte promised.

"You must look after Charlotte," the Viscount said to Alana. "If my aunt gets any idea that she is in love with my friend Shane, she will tell my mother and father, and I shall never be able to bring him to the Castle again."

Alana gave a little sigh.

"It all seems a terrible tangle, but I do want Lady Charlotte to be happy."

"That is what I want too," the Viscount said, "and somehow you and I must manage to see that she is."

He dropped his voice lower than before and went on:

"I am quite certain of one thing—if she were forced to marry the Prince, she would be miserably unhappy."

"I am sure that is true," Alana agreed, "and that is why I am here. But please, My Lord, you must tell me exactly what to do and help me not to make too many mistakes."

"I will help you all I can," the Viscount said, "but as far as the Prince is concerned, you will just have to use your instinct."

He paused for a moment before he went on:

"But if he is not bowled over by you, and I am sure he will be, then he certainly cannot have two eyes in his head!"

Alana gave a little laugh.

"Thank you, My Lord. That certainly makes me feel more confident."

"I think," the Viscount said after a moment, "you must now call me by my Christian name, and I will call you Alana. If you were really Shane's cousin, I would have met you a dozen times when I stayed with him in Ireland. And remember, you became friends with Charlotte when we both went there three years ago."

"Very well," Alana agreed, "but it seems somewhat . . . familiar."

"We have known each other since we were children," Richard said firmly, "and you must remember that, Charlotte."

"I *have* known Alana since I was a child," Charlotte retorted, "so it is not difficult for me."

It was impossible for them to speak intimately after that because the servants on the train offered them first coffee or a drink, then later provided them with a large and delicious luncheon.

To Alana, every minute was an excitement.

Only when finally, late in the afternoon, the train stopped at the Halt for Charl Castle did she suddenly feel cold, and the fear rising in her throat made it impossible to talk or laugh as she had done all the hours they had been travelling.

She also felt over-awed by the same reception that Lady Odele had received—the red carpet, Mr. Brothwick waiting to greet them, and the carriage which was far more comfortable and more impressive than anything the Earl of Storrington owned.

Then with her first glimpse of the Castle, Alana wanted to run away back into obscurity.

Never had she imagined that any private building could be so enormous or so magnificent. It was indeed, as the article she had read in the *Illustrated London News* had said:

A fitting background for its owner, who has the Royal blood of the Tzars in his veins and who

60

*lives more in the style of an Eastern Potentate
than an English Squire.*

Both Alana and Charlotte were silent as they
drove down the long avenue of lime trees and
reached the huge courtyard in front of the Castle itself.

As the footmen hurried down the steps to open
the carriage-doors, the Viscount murmured to Alana:
"Good luck!"

Shane looked into Charlotte's eyes and squeezed
her hand as the carriage-door was opened.

All four young people, as they stepped out, knew
that the curtain had risen on the first act of a play
which might turn out to be a comedy, as they hoped,
or else a complete tragedy.

They had all been primed by the Viscount on
exactly what to say and what to do, and as the Butler
announced them in the magnificent Salon where Lady
Odele and Prince Ivan were sitting alone in front of
the fire, Charlotte ran forward.

"Here we are, Aunt Odele!" she cried, kissing
her aunt affectionately. "We have had a wonderful
journey, and I do hope you will not mind that we
have brought with us Shane's cousin Alana."

Lady Odele was in fact already looking at Alana
questioningly.

"She arrived unexpectedly," Charlotte explained,
"because we never received her letter saying she
was coming to stay, and her luggage has been lost
somewhere in the Irish Sea!"

Before Lady Odele could speak, the Prince interposed to say:

"There is always room at Charl for one of your
friends, Lady Charlotte! And now may I welcome you
and say how delighted I am that you are here."

He spoke in a deep voice and with a sincerity
which Alana thought dispersed some of the tension

she was feeling, and she knew that Charlotte felt the same.

"Your Highness is very kind to invite us," Charlotte replied. "I have been longing to see the Castle, and it is even bigger and more impressive than I thought it would be."

"I am glad that it pleases you," the Prince said with a smile.

He held out his hand towards the Viscount.

"How are you, Storr?"

He then shook hands with Shane, who introduced Alana.

"My cousin, Your Highness, Lady Alana O'Derry, arrived just as we were leaving and I felt you would understand that we could not leave her behind."

"But of course not," the Prince said.

As he took Alana's hand in his, she looked at him with her large dark eyes and saw that he was exactly what she had expected him to be—overwhelmingly handsome and very different from any other man she had ever seen before in her whole life.

She thought it was not only his good looks that made him outstanding, but there was something compelling about him, something that seemed to vibrate from him, and he exuded not only a strong personality but an inescapable aura.

The Prince was looking at her searchingly and she guessed that it was the way he looked at all women, as if he were penetrating deep into their hearts.

She wondered what he expected to find and if he was often disappointed.

Then Lady Odele, who had kissed Richard, was saying:

"I too must welcome you to Charl and to the little party I have arranged for my niece."

There was no doubt, Alana thought, that the

word "welcome" was not sincere when spoken by Lady Odele, and the expression in her eyes was hard.

Then as they moved towards the fire she said briskly, almost as if it was a rehearsed speech:

"His Highness and I have arranged such a delightful programme for you, Charlotte. There is no-one staying at the Castle except ourselves, but there will be luncheon- and dinner-parties every day, dancing every evening to a Band brought from London, and innumerable equestrian amusements to keep Richard and Shane happy."

"That all sounds thrilling!" Charlotte exclaimed.

"I am sure you will find it so, and I really have scoured the country on His Highness's behalf to find all the young people of your age and of course Richard's. I felt sure you would not want a lot of old fogies like myself there to spoil your fun!"

As Lady Odele expected, Charlotte protested automatically at such a description.

"An 'old fogey' you will never be, Aunt Odele! Richard was telling us that your photographs have sold more than those of all the other beauties, including Mrs. Langtry."

"Is that true?" Lady Odele asked. "Who could have told you that?"

"I asked in three shops," Richard replied, "and they all said they had always sold out your photographs the moment they put them in the window."

"That is certainly very gratifying," Lady Odele said with a smile. "And now I am sure, Charlotte, you and your friend Lady Alana would like to see your bedrooms. And I suggest you have a little rest before dinner, because I expect you will all be dancing until the early hours of the morning."

"We are dancing tonight?" Charlotte enquired.

"Yes indeed!" her aunt replied. "We shall be fifty to dinner and the Band arrived early this afternoon."

Charlotte clapped her hands together and exclaimed:

"It all sounds thrilling!"

But she was looking at Shane as she spoke, and Alana knew that she was excited because she could dance with him.

"I am sure you too enjoy dancing," the Prince said to Alana.

"I do enjoy it," she replied, "but in Ireland we do not have the chance of learning many of the new steps, and I am afraid I may disappoint my partners."

"I am sure you will not do that."

As if Lady Odele was aware that he was talking to the intruder rather than to Charlotte, she said sharply:

"Come along, Lady Alana. We must find somewhere for you to sleep, and I suppose we should find you a gown as your luggage has been lost crossing from Ireland."

"She can wear my clothes, Aunt Odele," Charlotte said. "We are, luckily, about the same size, except that Alana is thinner than I am."

Her aunt did not bother to answer. She was already walking towards the door.

"Do not worry about not knowing the new steps," the Prince said, continuing his conversation with Alana. "I am sure you will have plenty of partners only too willing to teach you."

"I hope Your Highness is right."

She thought that the Prince was about to say something else, when she realised that Lady Odele with Charlotte beside her was waiting for her and frowning. She hurried towards them.

A little while later, alone with her niece, Lady Odele made her feelings quite plain.

"Now listen, Charlotte," she said, "I am not particularly pleased at your bringing an extra girl with you."

"Surely it cannot matter, Aunt Odele?" Charlotte replied. "The house is big enough for an Army!"

"That is not the point," Lady Odele said. "I want the Prince to concentrate on you and for you to concentrate on him."

"How can he possibly do that when you are here, Aunt Odele?" Charlotte asked in a deliberately guileless voice. "After all, you are so beautiful that I am sure he will have eyes for nobody else."

"I made it very clear to your mother," Lady Odele answered, "that the Prince wishes to marry again, and I know that you, dear child, will make him a perfect wife."

She paused for a moment before she added:

"If it comes to that, a man does not want a wife who is too beautiful and who attracts too much attention from other men."

Charlotte did not speak and after a moment Lady Odele went on:

"I want you, dear, to show him that you think him handsome and charming, which indeed he is. Listen to what he says and do show your appreciation of everything here at Charl. Girls are often tongue-tied, and it is such a mistake."

"I will try to do as you ask, Aunt Odele," Charlotte said in exactly the way that Richard had told her she was to speak and behave.

Lady Odele smiled.

"I am sure at the end of this little visit we will have wonderful, wonderful news for your father and mother, and I know, my dear, you will make a lovely bride."

Without saying any more, Lady Odele swept from the room.

She would have been very surprised if she had

known that as she closed the door behind her, her good, dutiful little niece put out her tongue!

A few minutes later Charlotte was in Alana's room, which was just on the other side of the corridor.

"Aunt Odele is furious that we have brought you," she said. "I thought she would be!"

"She is very beautiful," Alana said in an awed voice. "I am not surprised the Prince is in love with her."

"He can be in love with *Venus de Milo* for all I care," Charlotte said positively. "What I do not want is for him to be in love with me!"

Alana did not answer and after a moment Charlotte said in a different voice:

"I am frightened, Alana! Aunt Odele has it all fixed up. She said just now that when we go home I would have—'wonderful, wonderful news'—for Papa and Mama."

"I too am frightened," Alana admitted. "I think it has been just a waste of time your bringing me here. How could you imagine for one moment that he would look at me when Lady Odele is so beautiful?"

"Richard thinks you are far more lovely than she is."

"That is because she is Richard's aunt, and one looks at one's relatives differently from the way one looks at anybody else."

Charlotte clasped her hands together.

"Oh, Alana, if you fail, I shall have to marry him! You *must* try to make him interested in you."

"I will try because I promised you I would," Alana said, "but he is not like an ordinary Englishman. He is different, and that makes it much, much more frightening."

As she spoke, she was thinking that if the Prince had been like the Viscount, her task would have been easier.

She knew already, from the way Richard looked

at her and the note in his voice when he spoke to her, that he found her attractive, but the Prince was not English.

Despite his genial manner and his courtesy, she felt there was something hard and perhaps cynical about him, or perhaps it was just the attitude of a man who had tasted all the fruits of life and for whom there were no surprises left.

After a long consultation with Charlotte, having chosen the gown she would wear that evening from the dozens the maid had unpacked in her dressing-room, Alana was alone and she found herself thinking of the Prince.

He had been indeed what she had expected, and yet there had been something more.

For one thing, she had not expected him to be so vital, so alive, and she was sure too that he would be difficult to deceive.

"I must be very careful what I say and what I do," she admonished herself.

Even though she was supposed to come from Ireland and therefore be unsophisticated in many ways, the Prince might still be perceptive enough to sense that she was not what she pretended to be.

Yet, when finally she was dressed for dinner with the help of a very experienced maid, she thought that even her own father would have found it hard to recognise her.

The gown she had chosen from Charlotte's wardrobe was plainer than most of the others.

The fashion was for endless trimmings of lace and flowers, pleats, and ruchings and bows of satin ribbon.

But the gown Alana liked best was of course white, as Charlotte was a débutante. It had something almost Grecian in the folds at the front, while the sweep of the bustle billowed out behind her like the waves of the sea.

The bodice showed the curves of Alana's breasts, and the maid had pulled in the waist until it looked almost ridiculously small.

The whiteness of her skin was displayed by a low décolletage swathed with tulle over the shoulders.

Then as she stared into the mirror, she thought that because she was pale with fear, she looked almost ghost-like.

There was a knock on the door and when the maid went to answer it she brought back a large tray on which was arranged a variety of flowers.

There were bunches of orchids of every description and button-holes of gardenias and carnations, which were obviously for Richard and Shane.

Alana looked at them in a bewildered fashion.

"There are so many!" she exclaimed. "I thought there were only six people staying in the Castle."

The maid smiled.

"The gardeners wished to give you a choice, M'Lady. They'd no idea what you'd be wearing, and therefore they've picked many sorts of orchids in the hope that one would please you."

Alana laughed.

"I would certainly be difficult to please if I wanted anything different."

She thought for a moment, then took from the tray two arrangements of orchids. They were small, and instead of the familiar white, green, or purple, they were almost blood-red.

She thought the maid looked a little surprised at her choice, but she was too well trained to say anything and she took the tray back to the footman who was waiting for it at the door.

"I have an idea," Alana said. "Will you ask Lady Charlotte if she has some ribbon amongst her things? This colour, if she has it, otherwise purple or white."

Again the maid seemed astonished, but obediently she went across the corridor while Alana waited.

She came back with two pieces of ribbon in her hand.

"At first Her Ladyship thought she only had white, M'Lady," she said, "but then she remembered that one of her gowns was decorated with Parma violets and had little bows of ribbon attached to them. So I unstitched this."

Alana took the purple ribbon from her and skilfully attached one orchid to it.

"Now," she said to the maid, "will you tie it at the back of my neck?"

Her neck was very long; in fact her father had often said:

"You are like a swan, my darling, and as I used to tell your mother, a woman to be a perfect beauty should have three things that are slim and long, her neck, her legs, and her fingers."

Alana showed the maid how to arrange the orchids that were left in her dark hair, and knew she had not only relieved the whiteness of her gown but had given herself an almost Oriental touch of colour.

When she went to tell Charlotte that she was ready, she found her dressed in a gown ornamented with dozens of tulle flounces and caught with bunches of rose-buds.

It became her and was exactly the type of gown a pink-and-white English girl with fair hair and blue eyes should wear for a Ball.

"You are too pretty to be real!" Alana exclaimed.

After she had looked at her, Charlotte said:

"You look wonderful! And quite, quite different from any other girl I have ever seen. If we were in London, you would cause a sensation!"

"But we are at Charl," Alana replied.

It was impossible to speak more openly in front

of the lady's-maid, and as they went downstairs together they were both wondering what the Prince would think when he saw them.

Some of the guests had begun to arrive and had gathered in a larger Salon than the one in which they had been before.

There were a number of young girls looking healthy and countrified, and young men who would have seemed more at home on horses than in a Ball-Room.

The Prince was receiving them, but Lady Odele was making quite certain that they would know who was their hostess.

When Charlotte appeared, she exclaimed:

"Dearest child! I was wondering what had happened to you! Because it is your party, you were supposed to be downstairs before anyone arrived."

Ignoring Alana, she took Charlotte round, introducing her to everybody who was there already, pausing only to greet new arrivals and bring them immediately to meet her niece.

Alana walked to the side of the room and accepted a glass of champagne which was offered to her by a footman in a resplendent uniform festooned with gold braid and wearing a powdered wig.

Unexpectedly, the Prince came to her side to say:

"I am surprised at your choice of my orchids, Lady Alana."

"I thought them the most beautiful, Your Highness, from the very large selection which was offered to me."

"I have never known a woman to choose them before," the Prince said, "and I think I should be flattered that you have done so, for the simple reason that I brought them into England after my last visit to the East."

"They looked Eastern to me," Alana said, "and that is what makes them so attractive."

"You are interested in the East?"

"I have not had the privilege, as you have had, of journeying there, but I feel it has so much to teach us, if we will only listen."

The Prince looked surprised, then he asked:

"What do you want to learn?"

Alana made a little gesture with her hands.

"How can I put it into words, Your Highness? Perhaps the mystery of the Universe, the hidden knowledge which is not vouchsafed to ordinary mortals. Some of us sense it, but the East has always known it!"

The Prince's eyes were on her face and she thought now he was not so much surprised as astonished by what she was saying.

Then, before he could say anything, Lady Odele called out sharply:

"Your Highness!"

He looked round to see that there were four new arrivals for him to welcome.

When they went into dinner, Alana found that while Charlotte sat on the Prince's right and Lady Odele played hostess at the other end of the long table, she was relegated, despite her supposed rank, to a position far removed from the Prince.

She thought that if she had been genuinely Shane's cousin, she might have felt insulted by such treatment.

But she told herself with a little smile that it was not for her to criticise but only to be aware that Lady Odele resented her as a possible enemy, and that was a compliment in itself.

The dinner was an enchantment she had never encountered before.

The table was decorated with gold candelabra and other magnificent gold ornaments, and the first course was served on gold plate, which was something she had only read about in books.

71

In the Musicians'-Gallery, behind an ancient carved screen, soft music played all the way through the meal.

Alana wished to listen to it, but her dinner-partners were both sporting gentlemen who talked loudly and laughed even louder.

She forced herself to concentrate on what they were saying.

It was impossible, however, not to steal a glance occasionally at the Prince, sitting in a high-backed chair that looked, she thought, as if it should be a throne.

She wondered if he was enjoying himself.

She was aware that Charlotte was deliberately concentrating on the man on her right and making no effort to entertain her host.

Once or twice she caught the Viscount's eye, who was sitting on the other side of the table, and she thought that he seemed pleased with the way things were going, but she herself was not sure.

Already Lady Odele was on her guard, and she had the feeling that she at any rate would fight like a tiger to see that her plans for her niece were not disrupted by anyone, whoever she might be.

After dinner, when the ladies withdrew, Lady Odele said to Alana with a sharpness in her voice that was unmistakable:

"I should have thought as a débutante, as Charlotte assures me you are, you would have realised that the orchids you have chosen are very out-of-place, especially the one on your neck."

"I am sorry," Alana said meekly, "but they were so beautiful I could not resist them."

"Another evening I think it would be wisest for you to stick to white," Lady Odele said crushingly.

She swept away and Alana was left in no doubt that her appearance was displeasing.

It was, however, exciting when the gentlemen

moved not into the large Ball-Room but into another lovely Salon, from which the furniture had been cleared and which was lit by a huge chandelier in which there were hundreds of candles.

Here there was a string Orchestra, and as soon as they played the soft rhythmic strains of the waltz, Alana knew she longed to dance. When the Viscount led her onto the floor, she asked:

"How can I ever thank you for what has already been an unforgettable experience?"

"You look even more beautiful than I expected you would," he said, and she knew that he meant it.

"Lady Odele has already found fault with me for choosing to wear an orchid of this colour."

"I expect she saw, as I did, that the Prince was speaking to you before dinner," the Viscount replied. "What was he saying to you?"

There was a note that might have been jealousy in his voice and Alana replied truthfully:

"We were talking about the orchids. Apparently he is interested in them."

"He is interested in everything, as he can afford to be."

Alana danced with Shane, then with two other men in the party, and saw that the Prince was dancing with Charlotte.

Then as the next dance started she heard him ask:

"May I have the pleasure of this dance, Lady Alana?"

She found herself turning to him almost eagerly.

"Thank you. I feel in this lovely room as if I had wings on my feet."

"As long as they do not fly you away," he replied, "I am delighted for you to have them or anything else that pleases you."

Alana gave a little laugh.

"Why are you laughing?" the Prince asked.

"Because you say things which seem to come out of a book or a play and make me feel, as I have ever since I arrived here, that nothing is real but only make-believe."

"I assure you it is very real."

"Only to you."

"Why do you say that?"

She looked up at him with amusement in her eyes.

"Surely you realise that you are part of a fairy-tale, the *Arabian Nights* if you like. When I heard about you, I knew you could only have been invented by someone with a very fertile brain."

The Prince smiled.

"I think you will find that people who know me well know that I am real and, if you like, very human."

"I am told that we always have illusions about ourselves," Alana said provocatively, "and I am sure, Your Highness, that we could go on talking about your personal claims all night and still not come to any agreed conclusions."

"What have you heard about me?" the Prince asked. "And from whom?"

Alana smiled.

"Even in the Irish bogs the frogs croak about you, while the birds fly across the Irish Sea with pieces of gossip instead of corn in their beaks."

"Now you surprise me," the Prince remarked.

"That again is another illusion. You must be aware that wherever you go, they talk about you. Why not admit it and . . . enjoy it?"

The Prince laughed, then he asked:

"What do you think about what you hear? Or rather should I ask you what do you think now that you have met me?"

"What do you expect me to say to that?" Alana answered. "That I am overwhelmed, that I am stunned into silence with Your Highness's importance?"

"Now you are mocking me," the Prince said, "which is something I am not used to."

"No, of course not," Alana agreed. "I am told that everyone bows down in worship, but have you ever asked yourself whether it is you or your position which evokes such devotion?"

"Now you are definitely being impertinent," the Prince said sharply.

He swung her round in a waltz too rapidly for her to be able to speak for some time. Then when they were moving a little slower she said:

"I am ... sorry if I have been rude. You must ... forgive me."

"Not rude exactly," the Prince replied, "but perhaps I am not used to such frankness."

He knew, by the way Alana's lips curved, what she was thinking.

"I cannot believe that everyone I know pays me only lip-service as you insinuate," he said almost angrily.

"If I am being unkind in spoiling your illusions," she replied, "you must excuse me. You must put it down to the fact that I am not used to such exalted company and I do not know how to behave."

"I thought young girls of your age were sweet and gentle," the Prince said, "and looked at the world through rose-coloured glasses."

"Of course they do," Alana replied, "but sometimes what they see is so dazzling that they take them off."

"Again I have the uncomfortable feeling, Lady Alana, that you are laughing at me."

Alana sighed.

"I apologise, and I did so want you to enjoy your first dance with me. Perhaps now you will never ask me again."

"I shall most certainly ask you again, as I wish to continue our conversation," the Prince said firmly, "but I admit to being a little bewildered. You are not at all what I expected."

Alana made a little gesture with her hand.

"There are plenty of young girls here tonight who will say and do exactly what Your Highness expects."

"You know without my saying it," the Prince said shortly, "that I should find them extremely boring."

"Then you must not complain if I shock you."

"I am not shocked; 'curious' is the right word. How old are you?"

"The same age as Charlotte."

"I do not believe it!"

"All right, I am very old, but I have found the secret of eternal youth, which man has been seeking since the beginning of time."

"I am prepared to believe that your brain at any rate is a hundred years old!"

"So little? Then I must have at least a million more lives before I can approach Your Highness on equal terms."

His eyes narrowed for a moment.

"Are you talking about reincarnation?"

"I thought that was what you were referring to, only somewhat insultingly."

He looked at her and she felt as if they were duellists, weighing each other up before they raised their swords.

Then Lady Odele was beside them, saying to the Prince with an unmistakable edge to her voice:

"Really, Your Highness, I should have thought it unnecessary to stand in the centre of the Ball-Room if you wish to have a conversation with Lady Alana. Dear little Charlotte is longing to dance with you again, as she has just told me."

The Prince turned towards Alana, but already, as

if he knew what was happening, the Viscount was at
her side.

"You promised me the next dance, Alana."

"Yes, of course," Alana replied.

She smiled at the Prince.

"I thank you, Your Highness, for the most en-
joyable dance I have ever had in my whole life."

She thought that Lady Odele almost snorted, but
she took Richard's arm and he drew her away.

They walked out of the Ball-Room before he
said:

"What was happening? I could see something was
going on."

"I was doing exactly what you told me to do,"
Alana replied, "and I think the Prince was surprised
that I dared talk to him as I did."

"What did you talk about?" Richard asked curiously.

"Him and reincarnation."

"Good Heavens! No wonder he was astonished!"

Alana gave a little sigh.

She was thinking that what she had said to the
Prince had been familiar to her because she had discussed so much about the East with her father in the
past.

They had often argued over the subjects of re-
birth, the secrets that were reputed to be hidden by
the Priests of obscure, often forgotten religions, and
what Mr. Wickham had called "the esoteric language
of the Sages."

Of course, Alana told herself, the Prince had been
surprised that a girl of eighteen, a débutante from
the wilds of Ireland, should be aware of such things
and be able to duel with him in words.

She had read all the books on the East she was
able to obtain, and there was a special reason for her
interest which she was not prepared to tell anyone.

Lady Odele saw to it that the Prince did not ask Alana to dance with him again.

In the early hours of the morning Alana realised that neither Charlotte nor Shane was in the Ball-Room and she looked anxiously for the Viscount so that she could warn him that they were behaving indiscreetly.

Then unexpectedly the Prince was beside her.

"You are looking worried," he said. "What is perturbing you?"

"How could I be worried when everything is so delightful and I have enjoyed the evening more than I can tell Your Highness?"

"That sounds very plausible," he said, "but just now when you were looking round the room there was a worried expression in your eyes."

Alana did not reply and after a moment he said:

"You have the strangest eyes I have ever seen on any woman. They are very expressive—and yet—they are not."

"Surely that is a contradiction in terms," Alana said lightly.

"Shall I say there is something mysterious about them? They can express very eloquently what is on the surface, while at the same time they hide secrets that for the moment I cannot penetrate."

"And would you wish to?" she enquired. "I am extremely flattered by Your Highness's interest."

"If you talk to me like that, I think I shall spank you," he replied. "Just now when we were speaking seriously, I found it enthralling. Now you are being superficial and I cannot bear the artificiality of it."

"I feel when you planned this party you did not mean it to be serious," Alana answered, "so, like a chameleon I am trying to attune myself to the atmosphere in which I find myself."

"Then let me show you a very different atmo-

sphere," the Prince said. "I want to see your reaction
to it."

He put his hand on her bare arm to draw her the
way he wished her to go, and Alana thought that it
gave her a strange sensation she had not known before.

She could not explain it and she did not wish to.

She knew only that she wanted to go with him
and she had no compunction in doing so, because it
was all part of Richard's plan.

He guided her along a wide corridor and nearly
at the end of it opened a door.

The room was lit not with the gas-light that was
to be found in the rest of the Castle but with dozens
of tall candles set in elaborately carved gold candle-
sticks which might have come from some great
Cathedral.

They illuminated walls lined with gold silk which
were covered with Ikons.

At a first glance Alana knew they were very old
and very beautiful. There were literally hundreds of
them stretching from the floor almost to the ceiling,
some of them primitive and faded, others set with
precious stones which glittered in the candlelight.

There were also several which were of enamel on
pure gold and she thought that while they were not
the most colourful, they were probably the most valu-
able of them all.

She stood looking round and felt almost as if the
Ikons spoke to her. There seemed to come from them
a radiance or rather a vibration which had been all
through the centuries.

She believed it was the faith that had been
poured into them by whose who worshipped and
prayed to them until they had become vessels through
which the power of God could flow back to those
who needed it.

She sensed it and she felt the power and force of it until she forgot everything else, even the Prince standing beside her.

For a moment she felt as if she were swept on a strong wave of pure faith towards God Himself.

This was what she tried to find in her prayers and which she had always known was there—the irresistible radiance of the Divine.

She wanted to fall on her knees but the Prince's voice broke the spell that bound her as she heard him say very softly:

"Tell me what you are feeling."

With an effort she took her eyes from the Ikons to look at him, and she thought in the candlelight he seemed to be taller and even more vibrant than he had before.

Then, as if she was compelled to answer him, she said:

"You know there are no . . . words, but you . . . feel the . . . same. That is why you brought me here."

"I want you to tell me."

Alana looked again at the Ikons and answered in a voice he could barely hear:

"How can I describe the revelation of beauty to the mind? How can I explain a vibration which touches the soul?"

She paused, then went on slowly and almost inaudibly:

"God speaks . . . here, and I know you . . . hear Him too."

She turned her face towards the Prince and asked:

"How can it be . . . possible that you . . . feel as I . . . do?"

"That is something to which there is no answer."

Alana looked again at the Ikons.

"This is . . . what I have . . . always sought, and

80

now that I have ... found it, I know there are no horizons ... only infinity."

The Prince did not speak, but he took her hand and drew her from the room, shutting the door quietly behind him.

In the corridor he said:

"I think, for some reason I cannot comprehend, we are both bewitched. I do not wish to talk about it tonight."

Almost briskly he started to walk back the way they had come and in a few seconds they heard the chatter of voices and the music of an energetic polka.

Chapter Four

As Charlotte and Alana went upstairs after tea to rest, as Lady Odele had ordered them to do, Charlotte said:

"Come into my room. I want to talk to you."

As soon as they were inside and the door was closed, she said:

"Alana, I am frightened! Aunt Odele would not let the Prince leave my side all today and I feel sure that at any moment he will ask me to marry him—then I am—lost!"

Alana sat down in a chair, knowing that Charlotte was not exaggerating when she said Lady Odele had kept her and the Prince together almost by compulsion.

There had been no mistaking the anger in Lady Odele's eyes when last night she and the Prince returned to the Ball-Room, and even though the Prince immediately danced with somebody else, Alana knew the suspicion was there and that nothing she could say or do would change it.

When she had gone to bed she had lain awake for a long time in the darkness even though it was so late, thinking over what had happened and finding it all very difficult to understand.

It was not only the strangeness of her own reaction when the Prince had taken her to the room with the Ikons, but she had been aware that what she had felt in their presence was exactly the same emotion as they aroused in their owner.

She had no idea how or why she knew this, she only knew that what she had said when he asked her what she felt had come to her lips spontaneously. She had had no time to think, and it was as if he had forced her to tell the truth.

That he should have such a room hidden away in the Castle was astonishing in itself.

It did not fit in with his reputation of being a rich man in search of pleasure or with the picture of the brilliant, intelligent Cosmopolitan whom politicians and Statesmen admired.

Never in all the gossip about him or stories in the newspapers had there been any reference to a spiritual side of his character or that he was in any way religious.

"I do not understand," Alana said to herself.

She thought then that hundreds of women must have said the same thing, and he was an enigma like the Sphynx.

Even stranger was the fact that today he was obviously avoiding her.

What they had experienced in the room with the Ikons had not drawn them closer together but had seemingly divided them sharply.

She felt the difference as soon as they all met in the morning, when Lady Odele had already decided what they should do during the day.

"I thought this morning," she said, "that you would all like to visit the fascinating old Priory which is on the outskirts of His Highness's Estate."

She glanced out the window and said:

"It is a fine day and I know that you, Charlotte dear, would like to ride with His Highness."

The Prince, who had come into the room while she was speaking, had his eyes on Lady Odele's beautiful face as she spoke, and she flashed him an intimate little smile as she added:

"You will appreciate, Your Highness, how well Charlotte rides, and I know she will wish to see the finest horseman in Europe on your famous black stallion."

Lady Odele looked from the Prince to Shane.

"And you, Shane," she said, "will drive your cousin in one of His Highness's latest carriages, which are built for speed, while I shall ask you, Richard, to be my escort."

It was all cleverly contrived, Alana knew, so that Charlotte would be alone with the Prince.

When half-an-hour later they started off from the Castle, she thought that Charlotte looked so attractive in her well-cut riding-habit that it would be difficult for any man not to admire her.

Shane must have thought the same thing, because as soon as they set off down the drive and Charlotte and the Prince had galloped away over the Park, he said in a bitter tone:

"What chance have I against a man like that?"

Alana looked at him in surprise.

"You cannot doubt Charlotte's love for you?"

"She is very young," Shane replied, "and look what he can give her! I thought last night that the sooner I went back to Ireland, the better it would be for everybody."

"I cannot believe you really mean that."

"Oh, God, I do not know what I mean!" Shane cried.

"I have known Charlotte for some years," Alana said quietly, "and I am sure that she loves you with her whole heart, as she has always loved you. You

are part of her life, and if she lost you, I think it
would be like losing an arm or a leg, besides destroy-
ing her only hope of real happiness."

"Do you really mean that?"

He let the horses move more slowly, but as Richard and Lady Odele had driven on ahead, Alana
thought there was no hurry. What she and Shane
were discussing was very important.

"I have been thinking," she said, "that you and
Charlotte are facing this crisis in the wrong way."

"What do you mean by that?"

"I mean," Alana replied, "that even if the Prince
does not ask her to marry him, there will be other
men—her father and mother will see to that!"

Shane turned his head for a moment to look at
her and she saw the misery in his eyes.

"What are you suggesting?" he asked.

"I think you will have to be brave and make a
decision about yourself one way or the other," Alana
answered. "What we are trying to do now may come
off, but I know that you will still be tortured when
Charlotte goes to London to attend the Balls and
parties which had been planned for her before Lady
Odele produced the Prince."

"What have I to offer her," Shane asked, "even if
it were possible for us to be married, which I very
much doubt?"

"I am not going to make suggestions," Alana said
quietly. "What I am going to say to you is that you
must believe in yourself. My father always said that
if we want something badly enough we can get it, and
it is not a question of what we do but what we think."

As she spoke, she remembered the Ikons last night
and the feeling they had aroused in her, and she
added gently:

"Although perhaps it will embarrass you to speak
of it, there is always a Power that can help us when
we are desperate."

Again Shane glanced at her as if in surprise, then after a moment he said:

"I know what you are saying, and you are right. I have been faint-hearted and have not had faith either in myself or in Charlotte."

Alana smiled at him and said:

"Once you have decided exactly what you want of each other and where your real happiness lies, then any obstacles are worth surmounting, any difficulties worth fighting one's way through."

"You are right—of course you are right!" Shane cried.

The light had come back into his eyes and he squared his shoulders.

Then as if he must express his feelings by action, he drove the horses faster until they had caught up with Richard and Lady Odele.

The ancient Priory was little more than a ruin, and although there were some matters of interest in its antiquities, Alana knew that visiting it had only been an excuse for the Prince and Charlotte to ride together while the rest of them must keep to the roads.

When they returned to the Castle for luncheon, there were a number of people who had arrived with their horses to spend the afternoon trying out the new race-course which the Prince had built on the Estate and the jumps that only he seemed able to take effortlessly and with tremendous style.

"I hope you have told His Highness how much you admire the way he rides and how well he handles a horse," Alana heard Lady Odele say sharply to Charlotte.

"Yes, of course, Aunt Odele," Charlotte replied submissively.

"Remember, all men, however important, like appreciation," Lady Odele admonished. "Go and tell him now how brilliantly you thought he took that last fence."

Charlotte walked obediently towards where the Prince was riding his horse in from the course.

But before she could reach him she saw Shane talking to her brother, and she lingered with them so long that the Prince had dismounted and was busy inspecting several other horses that he wished to ride.

Alana saw Lady Odele's lips tighten and knew she was angry.

As if she had to vent her rage on somebody, she said to her in an icy tone:

"I hope, Lady Alana, that as you have known my niece for so many years, you will do your best to contribute to her happiness and not attempt to prevent it."

Alana knew what she meant but looked surprised and merely answered quietly:

"I assure Your Ladyship, the one thing I want is Charlotte's happiness."

"If that is true," Lady Odele said coldly, "then I hope you will not again try to monopolise His Highness's attention as you did last night. For your own good, I must tell you that I considered your behaviour extremely fast and not what one would expect of a girl of your age."

She did not wait for Alana to reply but walked away, looking, as she did so, extremely beautiful despite the expression of anger in her blue eyes.

When they returned to the Castle from the racecourse, their guests left and Lady Odele seized the opportunity, because she herself wished to rest, to tell Charlotte and Alana that they must do the same.

The Prince had already disappeared, and again Alana had been aware as she had at luncheon that he was deliberately avoiding her and had not spoken a single word to her the whole day.

"You must try to keep the Prince away from me, Alana," Charlotte was saying now. "I dare not be alone with him."

"It is not easy."

"Why not? He was obviously interested in you last night."

"I think he regrets what happened last night."

"Regrets?" Charlotte asked. "What do you mean by that? What did he do?"

Alana felt she could not tell anyone, not even Charlotte, that the Prince had taken her to the room with the Ikons. Instead she said:

"We talked on rather serious subjects, and I felt, in fact I knew, that for the moment he was interested in what I was saying. But now I am sure he feels he must keep to his original intention of marrying you."

Charlotte gave a cry of sheer horror.

"You cannot—mean that! Oh, Alana, that must not—happen!"

"It will not happen," Alana said quietly. "I am only telling you what I am sure the Prince is feeling."

"Whatever—happens," Charlotte said desperately, "I must not be—alone with him."

"I think that is wise," Alana agreed, "but I do not know quite how we can prevent it."

"If he suggests it, I suppose I can—refuse?"

Charlotte was obviously very agitated and walked up and down the room as if she could not keep still.

"I want to talk to Shane," she said, "I want to tell him what I am feeling."

"Shane knows, because he is feeling the same himself," Alana replied. "But you must be careful, Charlotte! If your aunt becomes aware of what you feel for Shane, I am sure she will make a fuss to your father and mother. Then they will not have him to stay with you and it would be difficult for you to see him anywhere else."

"You said you would save me—you have to—save me!" Charlotte insisted.

"I will try, I will really try," Alana promised.

"Come and choose a gown," Charlotte said, "and make yourself look so beautiful that he cannot help looking at you."

They went into the dressing-room where Charlotte's clothes were arranged in cupboards all round the room.

She pulled open the doors.

"There must be something here in which you will look outstanding and different from everybody else."

Alana did not say so, but she knew it was going to be difficult.

Tonight the party was to be bigger than that of last night, and she had learnt that tomorrow Lady Odele had arranged a large Ball which was to be held in the huge Ball-Room.

If on those two occasions Lady Odele was determined to keep her in the background, she might easily pass unnoticed, especially if the Prince was in his present mood of being determined to avoid her.

The more she thought of his strange behaviour, the more she was certain, with the same inner perception she had had before where he was concerned, that he was regretting the impulse which had made him take her into the room with the Ikons.

He was fighting against believing that they were indisputably attuned to each other in a way that was difficult to explain.

Last night she had known what he felt, and he too had been aware that the Ikons would mean to her what they meant to him.

Such an idea would seem incredible, Alana thought, to someone like Lady Odele and to most ordinary people.

But the Prince was not an ordinary man, and she knew from past experience that in many ways she was not ordinary either.

"He has turned away from me," she told herself. "He does not want to know any more . . . to probe any . . . deeper."

She remembered how he had said that she had secrets in her eyes, but Alana knew, almost as if he told her so, that he was determined to marry an English girl like Charlotte, who had no hidden depths or unaccountable perceptions.

She gave a sigh.

How could she compete with the rigid self-control the Prince obviously had over himself and a power that it was possible to use either for good or for evil?

"There must be something here that will make you look different and attract his attention," Charlotte was saying desperately.

Alana looked at the long line of white evening-gowns in tulle, satin, crêpe, and lace, all of which were virgin-white although some were decorated with coloured flowers and ribbons.

Then she remembered the ribbon she had worn round her neck.

"Where is your gown that is decorated with Parma violets?" she asked.

"I had that in the spring when I was in mourning for Grandmama," Charlotte replied. "But I told the maids at home to pack everything I possessed and they obeyed me."

She opened another cupboard and Alana saw hanging there several gowns of pale pink, blue, and mauve.

She looked closer, saw that there was one which was black, and lifted it out of the cupboard.

"Mama had that made for me for the first month I was in mourning," Charlotte explained, "but after that I was allowed to wear mauve or white."

"It' is a very pretty gown," Alana said reflectively.

It had been made for a young girl and was not

the sombre black that was connected with grief and tears.

Of fine net embellished with lace and black velvet ribbons, it was swept round in the front in the fashionable folds which accentuated the smallness of the waist and the largeness of the bustle.

At the back there was frill upon frill of net surmounted by a huge velvet bow.

Alana's eyes suddenly had a sparkle of mischief in them.

"I am going to wear this," she said. "It will certainly be a surprise, and I also have an idea."

"Black!" Charlotte exclaimed. "Are you sure, Alana? Remember, you have to look beautiful, much more beautiful than I."

"It will look fantastic," Alana said positively.

She put the gown over her arm and kissed Charlotte on the cheek.

"Cheer up," she said. "I have a feeling that everything is going to be all right for you and Shane."

"What sort of feeling?"

"A magic feeling like the one you attributed to Papa."

Charlotte's smile made her look radiant.

"Do you really mean that?"

"I really mean it," Alana replied, "and you know I would not say so otherwise."

"Now you are making me feel happy again," Charlotte said, "and if I cannot talk to Shane at the beginning of the evening, will you tell him if you have the chance that I love him?"

"I think he knows that already," Alana said with a smile, "but I will certainly tell him that you said so."

She went to her own room, where her maid was waiting to help her undress so that she could rest.

"I wonder if you would do something for me?" Alana asked.

"Of course, M'Lady."

"Then would you ask the gardeners who are preparing the flowers for this evening if it would be possible for me to have a number of small white flowers, in fact quite a large amount of them?"

"What sort of flowers, M'Lady?"

"I must leave that to them," Alana replied. "Perhaps they will not have many which are white, but please ask them to try."

"I'll tell them, M'Lady."

The maid looked somewhat disparagingly at the gown that Alana had brought from Charlotte's room, then she said:

"I'm thinking Your Ladyship'll need flowers to cheer that up! There's not many ladies'll be wearing black, not when they are dancing."

"That is what I thought," Alana said quietly.

Later, when the maid was arranging her hair, there was a knock on the door to say that the flowers had arrived.

When Alana saw them she gave an exclamation of delight.

The gardeners had not failed her. There were dozens and dozens of orchids, exquisite in their star-shaped, delicate fragility, pure white except for their stamens.

With the maid's help Alana pinned the orchids round the décolletage of her gown, and when she put it on she realised that it not only made her figure almost startlingly shapely it accentuated the translucent whiteness of her skin.

The orchids gave her a touch of fantasy and there was no doubt that she looked very unlike the ordinary Society débutante she was supposed to be.

With the remaining blooms she constructed a wreath that encircled the back of her small head like a halo, and this too made her look ethereal and at the same time amazingly beautiful.

93

"I've never seen anything like it, M'Lady!" the maid exclaimed. "I never expected a black gown could look as fantastic as that!"

"Thank you," Alana said.

"You'll be the Belle of the Ball, that's what you'll be!" the maid exclaimed. "But Her Ladyship'll . . ."

Alana was aware that the maid had been about to say, "Her Ladyship will not approve," when she lapsed into silence.

Because she was determined to help Charlotte by attracting the Prince's attention, Alana deliberately waited until she thought a number of the guests would already have arrived.

There would be over a hundred for dinner tonight, and she had heard the carriages coming up the drive for a long time before she finally took a last glance at herself in the mirror.

Then she began to walk slowly along the corridor towards the Grand Staircase which led down to the huge marble Hall.

As she descended, she told herself that she was playing a part not in a play but in Grand Opera.

How could she possibly be Alana, the help from the Vicarage, when she was dressed like a leading actress and deceiving one of the most notorious personalities in Europe?

Then like a cold hand sweeping away her excitement and elation she thought that perhaps her efforts would be in vain and the Prince would continue to ignore her as he had done all day.

In which case she would fail in her endeavour to help Charlotte and would return to the Vicarage as a failure, without even the consolation of her friendship with Richard in the future.

She was halfway down the stairs when she remembered what she had said to Shane when they were out driving.

"I must succeed! I *will* succeed!" she murmured

beneath her breath. "I am not fighting for myself but for Charlotte and for what is right and good. The power is there to help me . . . if I can but . . . use it."

She thought of the Ikons hidden away in the room to which the Prince had taken her, and she had a sudden longing to go there and ask for their help.

Then she knew that the help she needed was not only concentrated in the Ikons, it was within reach as it always had been if you could only get in touch with it.

She drew in her breath and as she walked across the Hall she felt as if she sent out a cry that winged its way towards the sky.

Then with her head held high, her eyes very large and dark in her small face, she walked into the Salon.

The Prince was standing just inside the door, waiting to receive the few remaining guests who had not yet arrived.

As Alana entered, her eyes met his and for a moment it seemed as if he recognised her not as one of his guests but across time and space.

She stopped still and neither of them spoke.

She felt as if there was no need for words. Something flowed between them which could never have been expressed by anything but music.

Afterwards Alana wondered how long they stood there looking at each other before Lady Odele interrupted by saying sharply:

"You are late, Lady Alana! And how extraordinary of you to wear black!"

With an effort Alana forced herself to look at the angry face of the Professional Beauty.

"I am sorry if Your Ladyship does not like it."

"It is quite ridiculous on such a young girl," Lady Odele snapped. "And so many flowers are ostentatious and extremely theatrical."

"You told me they were to be white," Alana replied.

She moved away, seeing with relief that the Viscount was hurrying towards her.

"You look marvellous! Stupendous!" he exclaimed.

As Alana took a glass of champagne which was offered to her on a gold tray, he added in a low voice:

"When all this is over, we shall have to make plans for your future. You cannot go back to the Vicarage."

Alana smiled.

"There is no alternative . . . and I am . . . happy there."

"It is ridiculous to think you can spend the rest of your life in the Vicarage at Brilling," the Viscount said.

There was a note in his voice which made Alana say quickly:

"Where is Charlotte? I must find her."

She walked away, aware as she did so that the Viscount was staring after her with a strange expression on his face.

Dinner was even more elaborate and more impressive than it had been the night before.

When it was over and the ladies moved into the Drawing-Room, Alana saw that Lady Odele had drawn Charlotte aside and was giving her some special instructions.

She knew by Charlotte's eyes that she was frightened, and she wondered what was being said, until as the gentlemen came into the room Lady Odele announced:

"Dancing will take place in the Silver Salon this evening and I have planned a special Cotillion for you in about an hour's time. There are lovely prizes, so I hope you will not miss them."

There were exclamations of excitement over this and the young guests went off towards the Silver Salon while Alana saw that a number of older people who had been included in the dinner-party tonight had stayed behind.

Lady Odele gave them one of her famous smiles.

"I know that you, Lord Sandford, you Judge, and of course Colonel Fawcett have no wish to dance, so I have arranged a surprise for you and our other friends in the Card-Room. I know you will all particularly thank me, because it is your favourite gambling-game."

"Baccarat!" the Colonel exclaimed before Lord Sandford could speak.

"Baccarat!" Lady Odele replied. "Go and start everybody playing, you hardened gamblers. The Prince and I will join you later."

As the young people went towards the Silver Salon, Alana hung back because she realised that Charlotte had not gone with them. So as not to draw attention to herself she slipped out of sight behind a large arrangement of flowers.

As the older people moved towards the Card-Room, she heard Lady Odele say:

"Before you join the dancers, Charlotte, His Highness is most anxious to show you the Music-Room. It is one of the most beautiful rooms in the house and I know you will find it fascinating."

As she spoke, Lady Odele, the pale blue flounces of her gown rustling behind her, smiled at the Prince in a way that seemed to have a very special meaning and followed the others towards the Card-Room.

Charlotte looked, Alana thought, rather like a frightened little rabbit. Her eyes, very wide in her pale face, seemed to watch the Prince as if she was mesmerised.

He stepped towards her, saying:

"Shall we do what your aunt suggests? I feel we have no choice but to obey her command."

Charlotte gave what was almost a cry of fear before she replied:

"Of course I would like to see the Music-Room, but Alana must come with us. Alana is really musical and she would be thrilled to see it, would you not, dearest?"

She turned to where she had seen Alana hide, as she spoke, and there was an appeal in her voice which was unmistakable.

Alana came from behind the flowers.

"I would love to see the Music-Room," she said, "if His Highness does not mind my joining you."

She knew as she spoke that the Prince contemplated for one moment telling her that he did mind as he intended to take Charlotte there alone.

Then there was a faintly mocking smile on his lips as he replied:

"Of course, I am only too willing to escort two such beautiful young women!"

Alana reached Charlotte's side and slipped her hand into hers.

She knew by the pressure of her fingers and the fact that she was trembling how terrified she was.

They walked out of the Hall and the Prince led the way down a wide corridor which was decorated with magnificent paintings and fine pieces of furniture.

As they went, they could hear the music of a waltz coming from the Silver Salon, and Alana wondered if Shane knew that Charlotte had been prevented from joining the other young people and, if so, what he was feeling.

They walked on for a long way, and she was sure that Lady Odele had chosen the Music-Room simply because it would be out of sight and sound of the party.

Finally the Prince opened the door of a room with a domed ceiling, marble pillars, and walls painted exquisitely with Chinese murals.

It was a lovely, romantic room, and as Alana saw

the huge vases of flowers and was aware of their fragrance, she thought it was obviously a perfect setting for a proposal of marriage.

Because Charlotte was so nervous she exclaimed almost over-effusively about the room.

"How pretty it is—quite lovely—and I see Your Highness has an interesting collection of musical instruments."

Alana had already seen the piano, which was a fine Steinway painted with pictures in the French style.

In another part of the room stood an ancient harp and against one wall was an exquisite satinwood spinet which she thought must be several hundred years old.

Although she was not looking at him, Alana was conscious that the Prince, still with a cynical, mocking smile on his lips, was standing looking at her.

He had brought her and Charlotte there, but it seemed as if, because his original purpose had been circumvented, he had no intention of behaving as a host would normally have done.

She was sure that that was what he was feeling. Then as she began to wonder if he would say that now that they had seen the room they could return to the Silver Salon, she gave a little start of surprise.

Lying on a side-table was a violin, and she had only to look at it to know what it was.

"A Stradivarius!" she exclaimed.

As she spoke, she put out her hand to touch it delicately.

"It is! How did you know that?" the Prince enquired.

"How could I not recognise it?" Alana asked. "Tell me about it."

She had forgotten to whom she was talking and it was a command.

"It was made in 1733," the Prince replied. "It has

always been in my family and is therefore undamaged and as perfect today as it was when it was first made."

"How wonderful!"

Without asking, Alana picked it up in her hands, then said in a voice that was barely above a whisper:

"If I could play this, it would be the most perfect thing that could ever happen to me!"

"You can play the violin?" the Prince asked.

"Of course she can!" Charlotte said, and added without thinking, "Her father was . . ."

Even as she spoke, she realised she was making a terrible mistake. But the Prince was not listening, he was looking at Alana.

"Why not play it?" he suggested.

"You mean that?"

Alana's eyes were brilliant with excitement, then without saying any more she quickly tuned the strings, tucked the violin under her chin, and picked up the bow.

For a moment she hesitated, then very softly began to play one of Mozart's melodies from *The Magic Flute*, which had been her father's favourite.

She knew as the first sound seemed to flow out on the air that the music she was making was very different from any she had made before, simply because of the master instrument that responded to her touch in a manner which she had never dreamt possible. The exquisite melody seemed to fill the room.

Then as she finished she could not stop, and with barely a pause she went on into a composition of her father's.

It was one he had written in her mother's memory and it was a cry of loneliness, of mourning.

It was a cry of love which could never die, a love which, because it was perfect, transcended death in the belief that neither life nor love could ever die.

100

It ended with a clarion call from a heart that suffered but in its suffering still believed.

It moved Alana tremendously as it always had when her father had played that particular piece, and as the last note throbbed away into silence, tears were running down her cheeks.

Only as she gave a sigh that came from the very depths of her being and took the violin from beneath her chin was she aware that the Prince was leaning against one of the marble pillars and Charlotte was no longer in the room.

For a moment it was impossible to speak, impossible to step back into the present from the other world into which the music had carried her.

Then she put the violin back on the table where she had found it and laid the bow beside it, and for the first time she was aware that her cheeks were wet.

She fumbled in her belt for a handkerchief, and before she could find it the Prince had crossed the room to stand beside her.

Taking a handkerchief from the breast-pocket of his evening-coat, he wiped away her tears.

For a moment Alana hardly knew what was happening, before the Prince's fingers, beneath her chin, tipped her face up to his and he looked down into her eyes.

It was then that she was aware, tinglingly aware, that he was beside her and that as he touched her cheek his face was very near.

For a moment they just looked at each other, until as if it were still part of the music, as if they were still in another world into which they had both been carried, the Prince's arms went round Alana and his lips were on hers.

It was perfect and inevitable, and there was no shock or surprise, only a feeling that this was meant to happen because it was foreordained and neither she nor the Prince had any decision to make in the matter.

Just for one second his lips were impersonal, then they became identified with the wonder that had been in the throbbing of the melody, the glory of the faith that the music had expressed, the love which surmounted death and was Divine.

Alana felt as if everything that was beautiful moved within her to become more intense, more rapturous than she had ever imagined it could be.

She felt as if the Prince's lips gave her all the loveliness she had seen since she came to Charl and what she had felt last night from the vibrations of the Ikons.

But now it was not only hers but his, and she knew that his lips became more demanding, more possessive, as he drew her closer and still closer, so that she loved him not only with her mind and her heart but with her soul.

How long the kiss lasted Alana had no idea, she only knew that when the Prince raised his head she was quivering with an ecstasy that was beyond expression, beyond thought.

She had ceased to exist as herself and was in a world that held only him and him alone.

Because it was so intense, she rested her head against his shoulder as if needing support.

He looked down into her eyes, shining now with the glory he had aroused in her, at her lips parted because it was hard to breathe, at the faint flush on her cheeks.

There was no need for words, she knew what he was thinking.

Then with a sound that was one of triumph, he was kissing her again, kissing her now more passionately, more fiercely, as if he was no longer god-like but very human and needed her as a woman.

Chapter Five

As soon as Alana started to play the violin and Charlotte saw that the Prince was listening to her intently, she backed towards the door, certain as she slipped out of the room that neither of them noticed her leaving.

She ran almost frantically back along the corridor down which they had just come, feeling as if she had escaped from a trap which had cleverly been baited by her aunt and which for one terrifying moment she had thought would keep her prisoner forever.

As she drew nearer to the Ball-Room and could hear the sound of the Band, she moved more slowly, trying to think how she could find Shane.

She remembered that her aunt had gone to the Card-Room, but there was still a chance that she might not be playing but might merely have settled her guests down at the Baccarat-table and moved back to the Ball-Room to see what was happening there.

Sensibly, Charlotte did not enter the Ball-Room by the main door but instead managed to find her way to the other end of it.

Here she surreptitiously peeped into the room to see all the young guests who had been at dinner dancing a Quadrille with exuberant verve.

Charlotte looked round for Shane, then with a leap of her heart she saw him almost opposite her, not dancing but talking to another man, a glass of champagne in his hand.

She looked at him intently, willing him to be aware of her. Then when she caught his eye she beckoned with her hand before she moved back into the passage.

A second later Shane was beside her.

"What is it?" he asked. "Why are you here alone?"

"I will tell you—everything," Charlotte said, "but let us go—somewhere where we will—not be—seen."

There was a frantic note in her voice which Shane did not miss, and, taking her by the hand, he drew her to a Sitting-Room where there was no-one except themselves.

As they went inside he turned to lock the door behind them.

Charlotte realised what he had done and flung herself against him, and as his arms went round her, she said:

"Oh—Shane—Shane, I love you! Tell me you—love me."

"You know I do, my darling," he replied. "But what has upset you?"

Then, as if nothing mattered except the fact that he was holding her close against him, his lips found hers and he kissed her until they both were breathless.

"I love you so—desperately," Charlotte cried when finally he raised his head. "If I cannot—marry you—I swear I will—kill myself!"

Shane kissed her again, then drew her to a sofa

104

and they at down side by side, his arms still round her.

"Tell me what happened after I left you in the Salon," he said. "I wanted to wait for you but I thought it would be a mistake."

"Aunt Odele made me stay behind," Charlotte replied. "She said the Prince wanted to—show me the—Music—Room."

She felt Shane stiffen, but he did not speak and she went on:

"I knew, even as she said it, that she had arranged that he would propose to me—there—and at the same time—I was sure that when he did, she would—announce it tomorrow—night at the—Ball."

"Without first consulting your father and mother?" Shane asked wonderingly.

"Aunt Odele is so determined for me to—marry the Prince that I do not think she considers anything except that he should—propose and I should—accept him."

"But you have not done so?" Shane asked.

"I escaped only—because I made Alana—come with us, and when we—reached the Music-Room she —started to play the—violin."

Charlotte almost gasped the words, as if she realised how near she had been to disaster. Then she went on:

"As soon as I saw that the Prince was—listening to her and not—watching me, I—slipped away and came to find—you."

"That was sensible of you, darling," Shane said, "but we cannot go on like this."

"That is what I want to tell you," Charlotte said. "I have escaped for the moment, but later tonight, or tomorrow, they will be just as—determined, and Aunt Odele will—contrive somehow—however much I— fight against it—that the Prince and I will be— alone."

"That is something that must not happen."

Shane rose from the sofa as if he felt he must be on his feet, and stood for a moment holding on to the mantelpiece and looking down into the fire.

Then he said:

"I want to ask you something."

There was such a serious note in his voice that Charlotte was aware that what he was about to say was of importance, and she clasped her hands together in her lap.

"What is—it?" she asked, her voice trembling.

"It is this," Shane replied. "I love you and as you know I have loved you for years. The only thing I want in my life is that you should be my wife. But, my precious, I have nothing to offer you—nothing, except my love."

"I want nothing else," Charlotte said quickly.

She would have risen from the sofa but he put out his hands to stop her.

"Do not move," he said. "I have to say this without touching you. If we face life together, if we marry with no money, you will live a very different way from how you have lived until now. I will work for you, I will do everything in my power to make you happy, but I cannot offer you any luxuries, and you already know how poor my family is."

"Do you think any of that matters?" Charlotte asked. "If I have to scrub floors and live only on potatoes, it will not matter as long as I can be with you. You say you have loved me for years, but I cannot remember a time when I did not love you. I belong to you. I am yours—and I could not let any—other man—touch me."

There was a throb in her voice and there was no doubt that the sincerity of what she said came from the very depths of her heart.

Shane looked at her, then smiled, and it illuminated his whole face.

"Then why should anything frighten us?" he asked.

He held out his arms as he spoke, and she sprang up to run to him and he held her so close she could barely breathe.

He kissed her until the room seemed to swing dizzily round them and they became part of the music which came from the Ball-Room.

After a long time Shane raised his head and said:

"I have to think, I have to plan, my darling, what we shall do. It is not going to be easy, but I do not believe there is any obstacle we cannot surmount together, and the most important is how we shall get married."

There was silence for a moment, then Charlotte said in a very low voice:

"Even if we—cannot get—married—I want to—be with you—to—belong to you."

Shane's arms tightened and he answered:

"I adore you for saying that, but somehow I will find a way."

He laid his cheek against her forehead and said slowly, as if he was thinking:

"I want you to go upstairs to bed. Undress quickly, in case your aunt finds that you are not with the Prince and tries to make you come downstairs again. If she sends for you, say you have a headache."

"What are you going to do?"

"I am not quite certain," Shane answered, "but I intend to find Richard, and when I have come to a decision I will get in touch with you, or he will."

"I understand," Charlotte said. "And, Shane, I am no longer frightened—but I shall just be praying that—everything will come—right for us."

"It will!" Shane said, a new, positive note in his voice.

He kissed her again, then he went to the door, unlocked it, and looked down the passage.

"I think if you go to the left," he said, "you will find a staircase that will take you up to the first floor, and from there you will be able to reach your bedroom without being seen."

Charlotte nodded, then as the music from the Ball-Room seemed to swell to a louder note, she started to run down the passage in the direction Shane had suggested.

He stood watching her until she was out of sight, then he took a deep breath and walked in the opposite direction.

* * *

The Viscount was asleep when he heard somebody calling his name.

He opened his eyes and as he did so he realised that he had been deeply unconscious, and it was difficult for the moment to concentrate on what was happening.

Then he realised that the candle had been lit beside his bed and Shane was sitting beside him, still in his evening-clothes.

"What is the matter?" the Viscount asked. "It must be damned late."

"It is after four o'clock."

"Did you wake me up to tell me that?"

"No! I have come to tell you that in an hour's time I am taking Charlotte away with me."

The Viscount sat up abruptly and pushed himself back against the pillows.

"What are you saying?"

"I am telling you what I intend to do," Shane replied. "Actually it is something I should have done before we came here, but now I can afford it!"

The Viscount swept the hair back from his fore-head and said:

"I may be very dense and thick-headed, but I cannot understand what you are talking about."

Shane smiled.

"It is not surprising. Do you know how much I have just won?"

"At Baccarat?"

"At Baccarat!" Shane replied.

"How much?"

"Nearly two thousand pounds!"

"I do not believe it!"

"It is true! And incidentally, I owe you twen-ty pounds."

As he spoke, Shane drew two notes from his pocket and threw them down on the bed.

"Why should you owe me that, and what has happened?"

"I will tell you exactly," Shane said. "The Prince intended to propose to Charlotte tonight and was only circumvented from doing so by Alana. When I was told what had happened, I realised that I had to act quickly and stop being unsure of myself as I have been up to now."

He paused for a moment before he said:

"It was Alana who made me realise that I was chicken-hearted and that because Charlotte and I loved each other nothing else was of any conse-quence."

"How did Alana make you realise that?"

"We were talking when we drove together this morning, and all day I have been thinking of what she said."

There was silence for a moment, and the Vis-count prompted:

"Go on!"

"Tonight when Charlotte told me how she es-

109

caped from the Prince, I sent her to bed and then went to find you."

"I was in the Ball-Room," the Viscount said.

"I never got to you," Shane explained, "because as I walked away from where Charlotte and I had been hiding, I saw Lady Odele come out of the Card-Room. Because I knew she was going to the Ball-Room and I wished to avoid her, I went instead to the room from which she had just emerged."

There was a look in the Viscount's eyes that told him he was beginning to understand what had happened.

"I stood just looking at the people playing Baccarat," Shane went on. "Then my Celtic sixth sense, or what Alana calls a belief in an omnipotent power, seemed to tell me what I must do."

He smiled at his friend before he continued:

"Of course, as usual, I had no money to spend, so I went up to your room and helped myself to twenty pounds that I knew you had stowed away in the usual place."

The Viscount grinned.

"It is always a mistake to trust even one's best friend!"

"I would have paid you back, you dolt," Shane replied, "but not as easily as I am able to do now."

"Go on!" the Viscount said again.

"I went back to the Card-Room, sat down at the Baccarat-table, and said to the Fates: 'It is time you gave me a break, and it is now or never!' So they obliged!"

"They certainly did!"

"Once I began to win other people's money, I grew more bold. Then the Prince arrived."

"The Prince?"

"I do not know if he was upset that Charlotte had escaped him, or whether it was something else,"

Shane said, "but he seemed in a very strange mood, and he started to play in what I should have thought was an extremely reckless fashion."

"That does not sound at all like him."

"That is what I thought. The older gentlemen began to take money off him and I did the same."

"Did I hear you say you won nearly two thousand pounds, or was I still asleep?"

"You heard me," Shane answered. "And by that time, as you can imagine, it was growing very late. In fact, it was only about an hour ago that we finished playing."

"What about my aunt?"

"I had the idea that she was perturbed over the Prince's behaviour. She came in several times to ask him if he would join the dancers in the Ball-Room, but he refused, and ignored anything else she had to say. Then when she suggested he should say goodnight to his guests, he told her to do it for him."

"He usually has such impeccably good manners."

"Tonight he refused to leave the gambling-table and did not even rise to his feet when Lady Odele said good-night in a very acid voice."

"I suppose he was upset at not being able to propose to Charlotte," the Viscount murmured.

"I do not intend to give him another opportunity," Shane said. "You must see, Richard, that this makes everything easy. At least Charlotte and I can keep ourselves for a year while we are in hiding from your father and mother, and I have something else to tell you."

"What is that?" the Viscount enquired.

"Judge Hudson was there tonight."

"Yes, I know. I met him before dinner."

"As he was leaving," Shane said, "I took him on one side and asked him if he would explain to me a point in Law which would help a friend of mine."

"What did you want to know?" the Viscount asked curiously.

"I asked the Judge whether, if a minor wished to be married and could not get in touch with her Guardian, who naturally would be her father legally, anyone else was entitled to give permission."

"What did the Judge reply?"

"He said in those circumstances it is possible for the girl's mother, her uncle, or of course her brother, if he is of age, to act *in loco parentis.*"

"I never thought of that," the Viscount said simply.

"I think the Judge was aware that it was a personal request," Shane said, "because before he left, he put his hand on my shoulder and said: 'Good luck, my boy!'"

"Now I understand," the Viscount said. "Do you want it in writing?"

"Of course!"

"And you are really leaving now?"

"As soon as Charlotte and Alana have everything packed."

Shane gave a sigh which was one of relief.

"Everything is even easier than it might have been. For instance, the trunks which Charlotte brought with her were all in a cupboard in her dressing-room. Like all women, she is determined not to go without her clothes!"

"Perhaps she realises that your money will not last forever," the Viscount suggested.

"It will last long enough, and I tell you what I am going to do, Richard."

He spoke in such a positive manner that his friend looked at him in surprise.

"I have never seen you like this before, Shane. It seems our roles for the moment are reversed."

Shane knew he was referring to the fact that

112

whenever they were together, it had always been Richard who led, Richard who made the decisions, Richard who organised everything.

"I think," he said quietly, "that knowing how close I came to losing Charlotte has brought me to my senses. In the future I hope I shall be more of a man than I have been in the past."

"Whatever you are," the Viscount said, "you know you can rely on me. But you were telling me what you were going to do."

"My father has some land he bought a long time ago in the very South of Ireland, and when I was thinking of somewhere to hide, I remembered that on the Estate there is a rather attractive Georgian house, dilapidated of course, but labour there is cheap and it will not be difficult to have it repaired."

He spoke slowly, as if he was seeing in his mind's eye what had to be done. Then he said:

"But what is more important is that it is a perfect place for breeding horses. As you know, it is something I have always wanted to do, and with the money I have won and no rent to pay, I will soon be able to build up a stud on which I am certain I can make enough to keep us both in comparative comfort."

"It sounds an excellent idea."

"I thought you would agree," Shane replied, "but nobody except you will know where we are until it is too late for your father to try to take Charlotte away from me or to annul the marriage."

"You know you can trust me," the Viscount said. "And now let me write the letter giving you permission to marry my sister."

As he spoke, he got out of bed and went to the beautifully inlaid Louis XIV desk which stood between the two windows.

Shane lit the gas-lamps and Richard drew a

piece of thick parchment paper from the red leather case embossed with the Prince's monogram which stood on the desk.

He wrote quickly, blotted the paper, and placed it in an envelope.

He handed it to his friend with a smile.

"I would have liked to give Charlotte away," he said, "but I suppose you will manage without me."

"I am grateful for your help, and I hope it will not be long before you will be our first guest at Derryfield."

"Is that what the house is called?"

Shane nodded.

"My father renamed it after he bought it, but to my knowledge he has not visited it for at least ten years. We should be able to live there for at least another ten without his being aware of it!"

"Then you will certainly be safe at Derryfield," the Viscount said with a smile.

As he got to his feet he asked:

"What happens now?"

"I am going to change, then as soon as the servants are astir at about five o'clock, I shall say that I have to leave for Ireland immediately and order a carriage."

"You are quite certain that no-one will tell the Prince?"

"It is very unlikely. He went to his bedroom after the Judge and the other guests had departed, and he was so preoccupied with his thoughts that although we climbed the stairs together he omitted to say good-night to me."

"I must say, I am not looking forward to being here tomorrow," the Viscount said wryly. "What about Alana?"

"She of course is coming with us as far as the station," Shane replied. "Your story will be that she and I had to return immediately to Ireland, and because Alana was upset at leaving so unexpectedly, Charlotte came with her to keep her company."

"I see!" the Viscount said reflectively. "Quite frankly, I would much rather come with you than stay here."

"That is impossible. I am sorry, Richard, but it would seem too extraordinary if we all left in a body."

The Viscount suddenly threw back his head and laughed.

"I cannot believe it!" he cried. "Here are you, arranging everything, giving me orders, and carrying off my sister in an extremely high-handed manner without even asking my permission!"

"You know I am doing what is right," Shane said, "and I cannot understand why you did not think of this yourself when we first knew what your aunt was up to."

"You have forgotten," the Viscount replied, "that if I had done that, none of those nice crisp notes would be filling your pockets!"

"It has all worked out for the best," Shane said confidently, "and now, Richard, go and hurry the girls while I pack my own things. I shall not be long."

* * *

Travelling alone in a Second-Class carriage towards Brilling, Alana thought that while she would never be able to forget these last three days, they would always remain in her mind as a fairy-tale, something completely divorced from reality.

Yet when Charlotte had awakened her—it seemed only two seconds after she had fallen asleep —to say that she and Shane were leaving in an hour's time and she was to go with them, she had felt that it was the only possible ending.

Now, for the first time, when she was alone, she

was able to think of the wonder and the rapture of the Prince's kiss, which had followed inevitably after he had listened to her father's music.

She had known that she had played on the Stradivarius what she wanted to say to him but for which there were no words.

It was impossible now to deny that he had not only awakened her heart almost from the moment she had seen him but that her soul too had reached out towards him.

She had known when he kissed her that he too was aroused in a manner that could only be expressed in music.

For one ecstatic moment when his lips had touched hers, they had known love in all its perfection—sacred and divine, yet human and passionate, so that it swept them up into the sky and yet was part of all the beauty there was on earth.

It had been love as she had always known it could be and would be if she found the man to whom she belonged, the man who was a part of herself because they had been together since the beginning of time.

When she had agreed to go with Charlotte to Charl, it had not been only to help her but also for another, very personal reason.

But she had never imagined for one moment that the Prince would be the man who, despite her resolution that she would never marry, would become an indivisible part of her heart.

It would have been impossible, knowing the love her father and mother had had for each other, not to be conscious of how it could be expressed in music, not to be aware that love as composed by the great masters was all part of the love which God had given man as a reflection of Himself.

She believed love could never be hers in mar-

116

riage, but it had nevertheless been a part of her living and breathing which she could not deny.

She supposed that she had known from the very first moment she saw the Prince that every nerve in her body vibrated towards him and told her: "Here is the man you seek."

She was sure that he must have known it too, known it when he deliberately took her into the room with the Ikons, known it when his eyes looked into hers, when their lips said one thing, their hearts another.

Even so, he had continued in his determination to ask Charlotte to be his wife, and she had circumvented him only at the very last moment by going with them to the Music-Room.

There, they had both been carried away by the wonder of *The Magic Flute*, and because all her life her father had talked to her of the marvels of the Stradivarius violins, she knew she had been very fortunate to play one.

It was something she thought she would never forget, any more than she would forget what had happened afterwards when the Prince had taken her in his arms and his kiss had reunited them as if they had never been apart.

Only when he kissed her until she had felt as if she must die with the sheer ecstatic bliss of it, did he raise his head to look down at her.

For a long, long moment they were both still.

She thought she could see a fire somewhere in the darkness of his eyes, before he took his arms from her and, still without speaking, walked from the room and closed the door behind him.

For a moment Alana could hardly believe what had happened, and she felt so weak from the emotions she had experienced that she had to hold on to the piano for support.

117

Then, a little later, she had no idea how long, she sat down on the music-stool and gradually felt as if she came down from a great height to the ground that was still unstable beneath her feet.

Later still, it might have been an hour or perhaps longer, she found her way to her bedroom.

It never struck her for a moment that she should go to the Ball-Room. Her only instinct was to be alone, not to have to speak to anyone, not to lose the last ecstatic rapture which seemed still to envelop her like a golden cloud.

Finally she had got into bed to thrill and thrill again to the memory of the Prince's lips, until reality became a dream and she fell asleep.

When Charlotte had awakened her and told her what she and Shane intended to do, she knew it was right.

What she and the Prince felt for each other was only the extension of the first night when they had looked at the Ikons together.

Apparently, this had only made him more determined than he had been before in his desire to marry Charlotte.

She could not understand it, but then everything about the Prince seemed incomprehensible, except the fact that she loved him and, although he might deny it, some part of him loved her too.

In that she could not be mistaken. It was as real as the fact that she breathed, or that her heart beat. It was as real as the Castle itself, and yet perhaps that was in a way only a mirage.

Whatever it might be, it was over now, the Grand Opera in which she had felt she was playing a leading part was finished, and she had a few hours to adjust herself to being, as she had been before, the "help" at the Vicarage.

The early-morning train on which they had travelled from Charl Halt to London had been what was known as the "Milk Train" and did not even possess a First-Class carriage.

There was, however, a Second-Class one which was empty because there were few passengers.

It was a very different way to travel from the manner in which they had arrived in the Prince's private train, but Shane and Charlotte were concerned only with getting away.

As they sat holding hands and looking into each other's eyes, it would not have mattered what the train was like as long as it was moving.

"The only danger," Shane said, "is if your aunt learns that we have left and telegraphs the Station-Master in London to detain us."

"Could she do that?" Charlotte enquired in a frightened voice.

"I very much doubt it," Shane replied, "but the first person who is likely to be informed is Mr. Brothwick, and if he is called at eight o'clock, that gives us more than two hours' start. It is also unlikely that he will think it necessary to inform the Prince what has occurred."

"Suppose the Prince rises early?" Charlotte enquired.

"We were very late last night," Shane replied. "Even so, by the time His Highness has told the servants to wake your aunt and she has given instructions to someone to send a telegram and it has been received in London and the Station-Master has begun to look for us, we should be on a train that will take us to Holyhead."

"I could not—bear it if we—failed at the last—moment," Charlotte said in a small voice.

"You will not," Alana interposed. "You will both reach Ireland, I feel it in my bones."

She smiled at Shane as she added:

"I told you that you had only to want something enough to make it possible to get it."

119

"I followed your instructions," Shane replied, "so, whatever happens now, it will be your responsibility."

"I feel very proud and very happy that you have been brave enough to grasp at what you both really want in life."

"Of course we want each other," Charlotte agreed, "we always have; and we will never, never have any regrets."

"I could never possibly have any," Shane said, "but I want to make sure that you feel the same."

"I am so happy," Charlotte said in a low voice, "that I want to dance and sing—at the same time, because it is so wonderful, I want to cry."

"My sweet!" Shane said, and put out his hands towards her.

After that they sat very close to each other, whispering, while Alana tactfully pretended to go to sleep.

Now, alone, she wondered if she would ever see Charlotte and Shane again.

The Viscount was a different matter.

When they had said good-bye in Charlotte's bedroom and Shane had gone downstairs to order a carriage and find two footmen to carry down the luggage, the Viscount had held Alana's hand in his and said:

"You know I will get in touch with you as soon as it is possible to do so."

"You must be careful," Alana said quickly.

"I will be very careful for your sake, because whatever happens, no-one at Brilling must realise you have been involved in what will undoubtedly be a scandal when it is known that Charlotte has run away with Shane."

"I would love to hear, if it is possible, that they were married and happy."

"I will write to you," the Viscount promised, "and somehow we must meet."

Alana shook her head.

"That will be quite impossible!"

"Nonsense!" he said sharply. "You know I have every intention of seeing you again, but I cannot just drive up to the Vicarage door and have the whole village chattering their heads off."

"No . . . of course not."

"I will think out a plan. Leave it to me, but we may have to wait for a little while."

"You must be careful with letters too," Alana warned. "The Post-Mistress always reads all the post-cards everyone receives."

"I will write in a disguised hand, and you had better invent a number of relatives who have suddenly become ardent correspondents."

"Please be careful," Alana begged again.

"I shall be," he answered, "and thank you for being so magnificent in doing everything we asked of you."

Charlotte, who had been talking to Shane, turned her head to say:

"We can none of us be too grateful, Alana. It is all due to you that I am not married to that horrible Prince, and as soon as we are no longer in hiding, I am going to ask you to come and stay with us at Derryfield."

"Of course," Shane agreed.

"Then I can meet you there," the Viscount said with a smile, "if we have not managed it before."

There was a look in his eyes which said a great many things that could not be said in words, but Alana knew she did not wish to hear them.

All she wanted to think about was the Prince, and yet to tell herself severely that everything that had happened with him was part of a fairy-story in which he was the leading character.

Now she had to close the book and go back to a normal life as if nothing had ever happened.

'At least I shall have something to remember,' she thought, but somehow it was cold comfort.

She reached Brilling at about tea-time, and carrying the plain, light carpet-bag with which she had left the Vicarage, she asked a porter if there was anyone else travelling there.

"'Tis no use askin' Oi!" he replied in a surly tone. "Ye'd better enquire outside th' station."

It was very different, Alana thought, from the manner in which he would have replied had she been wearing the smart travelling-gown and fur-lined cloak in which she had journeyed with Charlotte to the Castle.

Now she had on her own clothes, and they commanded no respect and apparently at this moment not even friendliness.

When in the Waiting-Room at the station she had changed from the clothes in which she had left the Castle, she could not, because she was a woman, help feeling a little pang of regret because her own clothes seemed so drab and dull in comparison with the elegance and luxury of those she had borrowed.

As if what she was thinking communicated itself to Charlotte, she said impulsively:

"I ought to have given you some of my clothes, Alana, you looked so lovely in them. But I did not think of it and now it is too late to unpack anything."

"You will need them for yourself," Alana replied, "and it is important to keep every penny of the money Shane has won only for necessities."

"Yes, I know that," Charlotte answered, "and I intend to be very, very sensible. But one day I shall have my own money. Papa will not be able to keep me from having what really belongs to me, will he?"

"No, of course not," Alana agreed. "At the same time, count the pennies! When one is poor, there are always extra expenses which one never expects."

Charlotte kissed her.

"You are so wise," she said, "and I shall miss you so much, even though I shall have my darling, wonderful Shane with me."

"I shall miss you too," Alana replied. "You have all thanked me, but really I have to thank you. I shall always remember you both and Charl."

She could not say it aloud, but her heart told her that the end of the sentence was:

"And for ever and eternity . . . the Prince!"

Chapter Six

Alana was bathing Billy in the flat tin bath which she had placed in front of the fire in the Nursery after carrying two heavy cans of hot water upstairs from the range in the kitchen.

She was late getting the children to bed because she had been on her own with them all day.

The Vicar and Mrs. Bredon had taken Lionel, their eldest son, and gone to stay for the night with the Vicar's mother at the other end of the County.

"I hope you will be all right, Alana," Mrs. Bredon said before she left, "and I have asked Mrs. Hicks to sleep in."

"I shall be all right without Mrs. Hicks," Alana said quickly.

"You could not stay alone here. That would be incorrect," the Vicar's wife replied reprovingly.

Alana thought she would have much preferred to be alone rather than have to cope with Mrs. Hicks, who was usually more trouble than she was worth.

But she knew that Mrs. Bredon was thinking

that the whole village would be shocked if she, an
unmarried woman, was in the Vicarage at night without a Chaperone, and so she merely smiled and said:

"Do not worry. The children will be good with
me as they always are. You enjoy yourself."

"It'll be a change to get away," Mrs. Bredon admitted a little wistfully, "but a family party is sometimes overwhelming."

Alana wanted to say that she had no idea what
a family party might be like, never having been to
one.

As if Mrs. Bredon realised that she had been
tactless, she merely kissed the children, told them they
were to be good, and went off with the Vicar.

It was a cold, rough day, and after Alana had
taken them all for a walk they roasted chestnuts over
the fire and had hot buttered toast and tea.

By bedtime they were all much quieter and ready,
Alana thought, to go to sleep, with the exception of
Billy, who, having slept after luncheon, was still
active and in high spirits.

Alana found it easier, therefore, to get the other
three ready for bed first.

The two eldest were at the age when they enjoyed reading or playing with their toys, and, once
she had insisted that they wash themselves and have
their supper, they were quite happy to go to their
room, which they shared with Lionel.

That left her only with Eloise, whom she bathed
first and who was now sitting in her blue wool dress-
ing-gown at the table, eating bread and milk heavily
laced with brown sugar.

Billy, on the other hand, ran round and round
the room naked before he could be caught and put
into the bath.

There, he splashed about like a small dolphin
and Alana was glad that she had a flannel apron
over her gown.

It was a plain gown which she had made herself, but in an attractive if serviceable green wool which made her skin very white and reflected in her eyes, adding to the mystery of them.

She had rolled up her sleeves above the elbow and was soaping Billy, while he made every effort to prevent her from doing so, when the door of the Nursery opened.

She thought it must be Mrs. Hicks who had come upstairs with a long-winded story about some grievance or other, which would not only take an inordinate amount of time to tell but for which there would inevitably be no answer.

"Splash! Splash!" Billy was saying, suiting his actions to the words.

"No more splashing!" Alana said firmly.

She picked up a big sponge and squeezed it over him to wash away the soap, and he put up his hands to try to catch the water, laughing as he did so.

Alana too was laughing when she heard Eloise say: "Why are yoo'se here?" and turned her head.

To her utter astonishment, it was the Prince who stood there, looking extremely elegant and very large and overwhelming in the low-ceilinged room.

For a moment it was impossible for her to speak, impossible even to realise that he was actually there and she was not imagining him.

She had thought of him so often, because she could not prevent herself from doing so, that he was in her life, in her very breathing, although without substance or reality.

It was not only every night when she was alone that she thought of him and remembered the wonder of his kisses and the manner in which she had felt she was part of him and he was part of her.

It also seemed during the daytime that he was beside her, and she thought at times that it was as if she could speak to him and he could answer her.

127

Now, incredibly, so that she felt as if a meteor had fallen from the sky, he was there!

Ever since she had left Charl, now nearly three weeks ago, she had longed irrepressibly for news of Charlotte and Shane and, although she tried not to admit it to herself, news of the Prince.

It was only yesterday that she had received a letter from the Viscount, which she had almost despaired of getting.

When she saw that it was postmarked from Paris, she knew why it had been so long in coming and why too there had been no talk about him in the village.

It was a strange letter because he had not started it with her name but had plunged straight into what he had to say, and she read:

> *I know you will be wanting to hear from me, but I have had little opportunity for writing, and very little to tell you. My aunt, as we all anticipated, was furious when she learnt that Charlotte, you, and Shane had left the Castle without her being informed.*
>
> *I told her, as we arranged, that Shane had received a telegram saying that you and he must return to Ireland immediately and that Charlotte had decided to go with you. I think she was suspicious as to Charlotte's real reason, although she thought it wiser not to say so.*
>
> *I could see she was doing her best to placate the Prince and to leave the relationship between them undamaged by such a precipitate departure.*
>
> *I pretended that I saw nothing peculiar in this, and I think on the whole she believed me. Anyway, as I did not wish to be embroiled in the row which would ensue when my father and mother learnt the truth, I decided to leave England for Paris, where I have been staying with some friends. I therefore have very little to tell*

*you, and I am sure you will know better than I
do what has happened at the Castle.*

*I must see you as soon as I return. Do not
worry about gossip—I will think of a way in
which we can meet without anybody being aware
of it, and I have a great deal to say to you.*

*I cannot forget how splendid you were in
what I know was a very difficult part to play, and
that is something else we must discuss.*

Take care of yourself.

R

Alana read the letter through several times and
thought it was disappointing.

There was so much more she wanted to hear, so
much more she wanted to know about Charlotte.

Strangely enough, although she expected the
scandal to break every day, as yet the village knew
nothing about Charlotte and Shane.

When she returned to the Vicarage, it was to
learn that the Earl and Countess had gone North to
stay with some friends in Northumberland.

They were not due back at the Castle for another two days.

It was almost an anticlimax to find that the people of the village were not whispering about what
had happened at Charl Castle, and Alana could only
imagine that Charlotte's lady's-maid had not been in
touch with Charlotte's parents.

Now, when she saw the Prince standing in the
Nursery, another idea came to her.

Perhaps something had gone wrong! Perhaps he
had come to tell her that Charlotte was in difficulties.

She did not question how he should know, or
why. She only looked at him as she knelt on the
floor beside the bath, her eyes very large in a face
that had gone suddenly pale.

"What ... is wrong? Why are you ... here?"

Her voice sounded strange and inarticulate even to herself, and the Prince walked farther into the Nursery as he said:

"There is nothing wrong now that I have found you."

"F-found ... me?" Alana repeated.

Then, almost as if she felt Billy was some protection against her own feelings, she picked him up out of the bath, wrapped him in a big white Turkish towel that had been warming in front of the fire, and sat down in a low chair with him on her knee.

He protested volubly at being taken out of his water, and by the time she had quieted him down and was drying him, she saw that the Prince had seated himself in an arm-chair on the other side of the hearth-rug and was watching her.

She was suddenly aware how very different she looked from when he had last seen her, and it made her feel inexpressibly shy.

"I'se finished," Eloise said from the table.

"Then say your Grace," Alana answered automatically.

Eloise was a pretty child with fair hair that complemented her fair skin.

With her small hands together, she shut her eyes.

"Thank-you-God-for-my-good-supper-please-may-I-get-down!" she said in one breath.

She did not wait for permission but slithered from her chair and walked across the room to stand at the Prince's side.

"Yoo'se bigger than my Dadda," she said conversationally.

"And you are smaller than Alana," the Prince replied.

The way he spoke her name made Alana feel a little flame of excitement run through her.

Then she told herself that the mere fact that he no longer prefixed it with "Lady" depicted all too clearly the gulf that lay between them.

Now she was no longer "Lady Alana" or even "Miss."

She was just a servant to be addressed by her Christian name and ordered to do the bidding of her betters.

"Have yoos come to see Alana?" Eloise asked curiously.

"Yes, I have," the Prince replied, "and I have been looking for her for a long time."

"Has she been hiding?"

"Yes, she has been hiding, but I have been very clever in being able to find her."

"She's here with us."

"I know that now," the Prince agreed.

Because Alana found his conversation with Eloise embarrassing, she said:

"Go and get into bed, Eloise, and I will come and hear your prayers in a moment."

Eloise was looking at the Prince.

"Yoos can kiss me good-night," she said invitingly.

Alana could not help a smile.

Whatever their age, she thought, they found him attractive.

It was like the stab of a dagger to realise how many women there were in his life. She was just one of them, only perhaps more foolish than the others.

The Prince had picked up Eloise and put her on his knee.

"You will be very pretty when you grow up," he said, "and there will be no need then to offer your kisses to any young man. They will all be asking for them."

Eloise was not listening. She was playing with the buttons on the Prince's coat.

"Do not encourage her," Alana said in what she

131

hoped was an ordinary voice. "I regret to say she is already an incorrigible flirt!"

"Why not?" the Prince asked. "It is a natural instinct in every woman to attract a man and to be glad when she is able to do so."

"I think you are generalising from your own experience," Alana said sharply.

The Prince laughed.

"I might have guessed that such a statement would evoke an argument," he said. "Put the children to bed, then we can talk."

Alana wanted to reply that they had nothing to talk about. Then she thought it would sound foolish.

By now she had put Billy into his night-shirt, and she picked him up in her arms, saying as she did so:

"Come along, Eloise."

"Good-night," Eloise said to the Prince.

As she spoke, she raised her arms and put them round his neck.

He kissed her, then said:

"Would you like me to carry you to bed?"

"Yes, please. Yoos are very tall and if yoos carry me I shall be very high off the ground."

Alana had already reached the door of the room where she slept with Billy. Opening out of it there was a small room, little more than a cupboard, which Eloise, as the only girl, had to herself.

As she walked into the room with the Prince following, it flashed through her mind that they might be husband and wife putting their children to bed.

Then she told herself she must be demented to imagine that the prince would ever do such a thing even with his own children.

As Eloise told him where her bedroom was, she saw him carry the small girl through the doorway, her arms still round his neck, her fair hair brushing his chin.

'I suppose this is a new experience for him,' Alana thought almost savagely.

But it somehow hurt her to see him doing anything so simple when she knew how very different his life was in every way.

She put Billy into his cot, tucked him up warmly, and kissed his cheek.

His eye-lids were already beginning to close as she lifted up the side of the cot and pulled the curtains to shut out the dusk, which was rapidly turning into night.

Then as she moved towards Eloise's room, the Prince came from it, shutting the door behind him.

"I have heard her prayers," he said, "so there is no need for you to trouble."

"It is no trouble," Alana replied.

She opened the door and looked into the room.

There were no candles but by the light from the outer room Alana could see that Eloise was tucked up in bed, her head turned on the pillow.

She shut the door again, to find that the Prince was watching her with a smile on his lips as if he mocked at her efforts to find fault.

She blew out the two candles in the bedroom and they went into the Nursery, where the light came from an oil-lamp standing on the table in the centre of the room.

Now that the children were no longer with them, it swept over Alana even more forcibly than it had before how different she must appear to the Prince from the last time he had seen her.

He had kissed her when she was wearing Charlotte's black evening-gown decorated, as Lady Odele had said, theatrically with white orchids that had also haloed her head.

Now with the sleeves of her gown rolled up above her elbows, with her hair untidy from bathing the children, and wearing a flannel apron which was the badge of office of every Nanny, Alana told herself that the Prince saw her as she really was.

Almost instinctively her chin went up a little and her eyes looked at him defiantly.

He walked automatically to the fireplace to stand with his back to the fire, which had a protective brass guard in front of it on which were drying several pairs of socks that Alana had washed earlier in the day.

The bath was at his feet and the two towels which had dried the children lay beside it.

She wanted to pick them up, then refrained from doing so.

The sooner the Prince said what had to be said and left, the better.

She had known an irrepressible joy and her heart had leapt at the sight of him, but she now felt an agony because this was how he would remember her, and not as she had looked and been when he had kissed her in the Music-Room at Charl Castle.

As he did not speak, she asked:

"Why . . . have you come . . . here?"

"To talk to you."

Even as he spoke, she added in an agitated voice:

"How . . . can you have . . . found me? Who told you . . . where I was?"

"Charlotte, as it happens."

Alana stared at him wide-eyed.

"Charlotte? I do not believe you!"

"It is true, although she was reluctant to do so until I blackmailed her into doing what I wanted."

"Blackmailed?"

Alana spoke the word in horror, but the Prince was smiling.

"Come and sit down and I will tell you all about it. I am sure you are curious."

She was curious, Alana admitted to herself. At

the same time, it was an order and she knew she had to obey him.

Hardly thinking of what she was doing, she untied the tape which held the flannel apron round her waist and put it down on a chair. Then she pulled down the sleeves of her gown and fastened them neatly at the wrists.

She was uncomfortably aware that the Prince was watching her, and with a nervous little gesture she put her hands up to her hair before she seated herself on a chair opposite the one he had occupied before.

Because he was still standing, she had to tip her head back to look up at him as she asked:

"You have . . . seen Charlotte?"

"Yes."

"She is . . . married?"

It seemed for the moment the most important question of all, and as if the Prince understood her anxiety, he was smiling as he replied:

"Very much so. I have never seen two people so happy."

"How did you . . . find them?"

"If I make up my mind to do something, I am invariably successful," the Prince said. "I was sure that Charlotte and Shane had run away to get married."

Alana gave a little gasp.

"You . . . knew that?"

"Shall I say that I not only have eyes in my head but, as you know better than anybody else, an instinct that cannot be denied and is invariably correct."

"So you . . . guessed they . . . loved each other!"

"It was obvious to me as soon as I saw them together."

"Then why . . . ?"

Alana stopped.

135

She felt that what she was going to say would be impertinent besides being too intimate, but there was really no need for words between them, for the Prince said:

"That is just what I am going to explain to you. But what I had expected was to find you at Derryfield with Charlotte and your supposed cousin."

Alana drew in her breath.

"How did Charlotte . . . explain my . . . absence?"

"She tried to convince me at first that you had left for your home which was in another part of Ireland. But again that instinct, which you and I both have, told me that she was not speaking the truth."

"You . . . you said you . . . blackmailed her into . . . telling the truth."

"Perhaps 'bribed' would be a prettier word, and indeed more accurate," the Prince replied.

"Bribed?" Alana repeated. "Or did you threaten her:"

Her voice was accusing.

"No, I did not resort to anything so unpleasant. There was really no need. I merely made it clear, after the first shock of seeing me was over, that I was prepared to help Shane."

Alana looked up at him.

"You would . . . really help him . . . you mean in breeding horses?"

"I have bought quite a number from him."

"That was kind, really very kind of you," Alana cried. "If he can support Charlotte, then I am sure her father will forgive her for running away and everything will be all right in the future."

"That is what I thought," the Prince agreed. "At the same time, I made your address a condition of sale!"

It flashed through Alana's mind that in a way Charlotte had betrayed her trust and she might at least have warned her.

As if the Prince again was aware of what she was thinking, he said:

"You will understand better when I tell you why I wanted to see you."

As he spoke, he sat down in the chair opposite her, and it struck her that he seemed entirely at ease and at home even in such an unlikely place as an untidy Nursery.

But, because she still felt shy, she said automatically:

"You should . . . not have . . . come here."

"Why not?"

"The Vicar and Mrs. Bredon are . . . away and the village will . . . talk."

"Do you really mind if they do?"

"Of course! I have to live here."

It struck Alana what a great deal of gossip there would be if it was known that Prince Ivan Katinouski of Charl Castle had called to see her.

How could she explain his presence?

She could almost hear the news of his visit running like wildfire from cottage to cottage and from farm to farm, and the whispered constructions that would be put upon it.

"Please . . . say quickly what you have to say . . . and go," she said in a low voice.

"If I do obey you," the Prince replied, "without telling you why I have come, would you not wonder all your life what it was you had not heard?"

"Y-yes . . . of course," Alana admitted. "But you have no . . . idea what it is like to . . . live in a small . . . village."

"You certainly do not behave like a villager," he said, "and you certainly did not look like one when I last saw you."

"I was . . . acting a part," Alana said defiantly. "I was wearing Charlotte's gowns and Your Highness's orchids. Now you see me . . . as I really . . . am."

"I wonder," the Prince said. "You would be the first to tell me that it is not what people look like but what they think that matters. It was with our brains that we talked when you were at the Castle, and also with our instincts."

He spoke the words very softly, and, because Alana felt an irrepressible emotional reaction, she said quickly:

"Tell me why you have come."

"It is rather a long story," the Prince said, "and you must forgive me if I start in 1835."

Alana looked at him in perplexity and he explained:

"That was the year my father, having quarrelled with Tzar Nicholas, left Russia."

"I have heard that he hated the Tzar," Alana said in a low voice.

"It was not surprising. Nicholas was a monster, a tyrant; a man so cruel that the horrors of his reign are deeply ingrained in all those who endured it."

"But your father escaped."

"He left, saying he loathed Russia and everything to do with it," the Prince replied. "He came to England and was clever enough to bring with him his huge fortune and many of his treasured possessions."

He paused for a moment to say:

"The Ikons I showed you at the Castle belonged to my father. They had never been unpacked from the time he left Russia until I bought the Castle."

"You had never seen them!" Alana exclaimed.

The Prince shook his head.

"Not until I had constructed that room especially for them, and you were one of the first people besides myself to enter it."

Alana looked at him wide-eyed, but he went on:

"As perhaps you know, my father married the Duke of Warminster's daughter, and when I was

138

born I was brought up to be English in every possible way. I was sent to English Schools and to an English University. I even served for three years in an English Regiment before my father died. Then I realised that as my own master I need no longer conform entirely to the dictates he had imposed upon me ever since I was a child."

The Prince paused for a moment before he said in a voice that seemed almost to ring out in the Nursery:

"But I personally loathed and detested everything that was Russian!"

There was silence. Then Alana said:

"But even so . . . you were still half-Russian."

"Do you suppose I was not aware of that?" the Prince asked almost harshly. "I fought against every emotion which I knew conflicted with the English side of my character. Most of all, I fought against what you call 'instinct'—those feelings, those perceptions, and the inner knowledge which no Englishman is capable of feeling or understanding."

He gave a deep sigh.

"I am telling you this so that you will understand when I tell you that I made a terrible mistake in marrying not, as my father would have wished me to do, an English girl, but a Hungarian."

"But you . . . loved her?"

Alana had the feeling that the question was impertinent, but it came from her lips instinctively.

"Yes, I loved her," the Prince admitted. "At least I thought I did. She was very beautiful, very wild, a dashing horsewoman, and we seemed to have a great deal in common."

His eyes in the light from the oil-lamp were bleak as he went on:

"A few weeks after I was married, I realised I had made a mistake, but it was too late and there was nothing I could do about it. Then, as you know, she was injured in a riding accident which was entirely her own fault and should never have happened."

"It was very . . . tragic," Alana said softly.

"It was not really tragic for me," the Prince said, "because I was free to roam the world, to do as I wished, to have, as you have doubtless heard, a great number of love-affairs."

His lips curled mockingly for a moment as he added:

"How many falsehoods lie in that word 'love.'"

There was great bitterness in the way he spoke, and Alana could think only of the beautiful women who had thrown themselves at his feet, women like Lady Odele, who in her own way had given him her heart, even if it was a shallow one.

"Yes, there were women and plenty of them," the Prince said, "but I was always determined that my wife should be English and as conventional and unimaginative as my mother had been. It was what my father had wanted, and I wanted the same thing."

He looked at Alana for a long moment, then he said:

"Because my wife died only a short time ago, I had to wait longer than I intended. But as soon as I was free, I told myself I would now plan my life in the way that I had always intended. I would have a family who would only be one-quarter Russian, and that part of my blood that I had always hated would be gradually eliminated down the generations."

Because he spoke so positively in a way which seemed to vibrate from him, Alana clasped her hands together, but she did not speak.

"Then you know what happened," the Prince said in a different tone of voice. "You came to the Castle with the girl whom Lady Odele had chosen as my bride-to-be, and awoke within me all the feelings I had denied and thrust from me ever since I had been a young boy."

"It was . . . not intentional."

"I know that," the Prince replied. "But as soon as we looked at each other, you knew as well as I do that something passed between us that was different from anything I had experienced with any other person in my whole life, and I cannot believe that you have ever felt it with anybody except me."

Alana's lips moved, but as if she thought it would be a mistake to interrupt his thoughts, she said nothing, and the Prince went on:

"God knows it is difficult to explain to you why I took you into the room with the Ikons. It was, I think, because I wanted to prove to myself I was not imagining what you were making me feel."

"Anyone would have been . . . moved, as I was, by the . . . beauty of them," Alana said hesitatingly.

"You know that is not true," the Prince said sharply. "What you felt and what I felt was quite different from the reaction of any ordinary person. They would have admired their beauty and they would have appreciated their value, but do you think they would have felt as you did—the power, the vibrations of them, or, as you said yourself, God speaking through them?"

Alana looked down at her clasped hands and the Prince went on:

"I knew when we left that room that you had frightened me in a way I had never been frightened before."

"Frightened . . . you?"

"But of course! Frightened that everything that was Russian within me was coming to the surface. It was like a volcano erupting through the outer crust which I had always believed I held under control but which crumbled at your touch."

141

"I am sure . . . that is not . . . true."

"What I am telling you is the truth," the Prince said. "And I hated you because you disturbed me so profoundly."

"You . . . avoided me the . . . next day."

"I meant to. I could not speak to you, but do you suppose I was not vividly conscious of you every second, every minute? I felt it was as if, like the Ikons, you drew me by a kind of mesmerism and I could not escape."

Alana thought that that was exactly how she had felt about the Prince.

He was mesmeric and she knew that that was the reason why she could not cease thinking of him, could not put him out of her mind.

"I told myself I would be free of you," the Prince went on. "I had only to stick to the original plan that Lady Odele had made for me and marry her niece Charlotte. Once she was my wife, you would go back to Ireland and I would never see you again."

He gave a little laugh.

"I had underestimated again the force and power of the Russian side of my character. The volcano was still raging, the flames leaping higher and higher, and when you played to me on the violin you told me what you were feeling and thinking, and there was nothing I could do but—surrender."

The Prince spoke the last words very softly and Alana felt as if her heart turned over in her breast.

"I knew then," he said, "that love is something that cannot be denied, cannot be refused. I had found love when I least expected it, after all the long years of thinking that the real ecstasy and wonder of it was something that would never exist for me."

"Why . . . should you have . . . thought that?"

"Because," the Prince said quietly, "the sort of

love I wanted and needed was a love that only a Russian could desire."

He made a gesture with his hands almost of helplessness before he said:

"How can I explain? To a Russian, love is part of the soul. In other countries, it is an emotion of the heart, but to a Russian it is part of his belief in God, a part so intrinsically wrapped up with his faith and the very breath he draws that it can never take second place to anything in his life."

The way the Prince spoke was very moving, and Alana knew it was what she too had always felt and believed.

His eyes were on her face as if he read her thoughts. Then he said:

"Now you understand that I have come here to ask you if you will be my wife."

For a moment Alana felt that she could not have heard him aright.

Then as she looked into his eyes, she knew that he had said it and it flashed through her mind that it was the most incredibly, unbelievably wonderful thing that had ever happened to her.

Prince Ivan Katinouski had asked if she would marry him!

Without realising she was doing so, she rose to her feet and held on to the high Nursery guard as if it gave her support as she said:

"D-do you ... realise what you are ... s-saying?"

"Of course I realise it!" the Prince answered. "It drove me nearly mad trying to find you! When Charlotte told me you were not Shane's cousin and that after they had inveigled you into coming to the Castle to divert my attention from Charlotte you had disappeared, I thought I should go insane."

"They said you would not ... find me?" Alana asked.

"They said I would not only be unable to do so but it would be a great mistake if I did."

"That ... is what ... it is."

Alana drew in her breath.

"I am very honoured that Your Highness should have ... sought me out and that you should have ... asked me to ... marry you ... but my answer is ... no."

"No?"

The Prince ejaculated the word almost like a pistol-shot.

"No," Alana repeated, although her voice trembled. "And now, Your Highness, please go! There is nothing more to say, and I am sure that one day you will find someone who will be ... suitable as your wife and will make you ... happy."

The Prince did not move, he merely said, looking at her as she stared down at the fire:

"Do you imagine for one moment that I will accept your decision or allow you to refuse me?"

He saw her give a little quiver as if with fear, then she said:

"It is ... something you ... have to do."

"Why?"

"Because I cannot marry you. In fact ... I shall never ... marry anybody."

"Why should you say that?" the Prince asked. "How can you possibly make such an absurd statement?"

"It is true ... but I do not wish to talk about it."

"Do you really think I would accept your decision without an explanation? And a very convincing one?"

Alana turned to look at him, and he saw an expression in her eyes which he thought made her suddenly look tragic and at the same time infinitely pathetic.

"You are hiding something else. I suppose I always knew there was something mysterious about you. When Charlotte told me who you were, I thought that was the reason for what I felt. Now I know it is something different."

"Please ... please," Alana begged, "do not use your instinct where ... I am concerned. Just ... go away and leave me alone ... there is nothing more to say."

"That is impossible!"

"Please ... I beg of you."

"Then I must refuse your plea," the Prince replied, "not only for my sake but for yours. You know as well as I do that we belong to each other, Alana, and I can make you happy."

He smiled in a manner which was very beguiling as he said:

"Now I am being Russian, but I am convinced that we shall be incredibly happy together in what, surprisingly as far as the rest of the world is concerned, will be a perfect marriage."

"B-but I ... cannot ... marry you."

There was a sob on the words that the Prince did not miss.

"Why not, my darling?" he asked. "You know that I love you and I know already that you love me. You told me what you felt in music, and when I kissed your lips you gave me your soul."

"But ... I still cannot ... marry you," Alana murmured.

"Tell me why!" the Prince insisted. "I must know. Do you imagine I could go away and spend the rest of my life in agony, ignorance, and doubt? My precious, be practical. We may travel together towards the stars, but we still have to live on this earth. You have already made me suffer more than any man should be expected to endure in one lifetime."

Alana gave a little sigh and he thought she was near to tears.

Then she said:

"Very well . . . I will tell you . . . then you will . . . understand that not only can I not marry you, but you will no longer . . . wish to marry me."

The Prince merely smiled very gently and she knew he did not believe her.

"I suppose," she said, "you will not . . . accept the . . . obvious reason . . . that I am . . . as you see, a paid helper in a Vicarage; an orphan with no money . . . no background; unsuitable in every way to be the . . . wife of Prince Ivan Katinouski."

"You forget," he replied, "that I have also seen you act the part of a Society Lady so brilliantly, so flawlessly, that it could not have been pretence but was something completely natural to you."

His voice died away into silence, then before Alana could speak he added:

"Feeling as we do for each other, it would not matter if you had been born in the gutter and brought up in a slum. It would not matter who your parents were, or what menial task you have had to perform in order to live. You are mine, Alana, mine since the beginning of time, and mine for the rest of eternity, and whether you marry me or not, that is an indisputable fact!"

Alana was trembling at the passion in his words and after a moment he said very quietly:

"I am not touching you as I want to do. I am not taking an unfair advantage, because I know if I kissed you again there would really be no need for words. We would be joined as we were before, and there would be no more arguments as to whether or not you were mine."

His voice deepened as he said:

"I want to kiss you, God knows I want it, and it is with the greatest difficulty that I am restraining myself. So hurry, my precious, and say what you have to say before I take you in my arms."

Now Alana put up her hands almost as if he had moved towards her and she was fending him off.

Then as if she could not bear to look at him and see the love in his eyes, she shut her own before she said in a voice he could barely hear:

"My father, as I expect Charlotte told you, was Irving Wickham, a music-teacher . . . but my mother was . . . Princess Natasha Katinouski!"

There was silence as the Prince stared at her. Then he said:

"My relative?"

"Your father's cousin."

"She must have married your father long after mine had left Russia."

"Many years later."

"Tell me exactly what happened."

Alana drew a deep breath.

"My grandfather, much to the annoyance of the Wickham family, was extremely musical. He refused to be interested in his father's Estates, but attached himself to one of the big Orchestras in the North and became a very well-known Conductor, calling himself Axel Alstone."

Alana paused almost as if she thought the Prince might say he had heard of him. Then, as he did not speak, she went on:

"It was arranged that my grandfather should take his Orchestra on a tour of Europe, ending in St. Petersburg."

"What year was this?" the Prince interposed.

"In 1858, three years after Tzar Nicholas was dead and Alexander II had come to the throne."

"A very different Tzar!"

"So I believe," Alana agreed, "but that did not help my mother."

"Why not?"

"My grandfather was taken ill in Warsaw. My father, who was the First Violin, rather than disappoint the other members of the Orchestra, took his father's place and they went on to St. Petersburg."

"It was there, I suppose," the Prince said, "that he met my father's cousin, your mother?"

"She was very young and more beautiful, my father told me, than anyone he had ever seen before in his life. She asked him to give her music-lessons, and, as you know, it was fashionable amongst the Russian aristocracy at that time to have distinguished music-teachers, and the majority of them were French."

"So they fell in love as we fell in love," the Prince finished softly.

"They ... fell in love," Alana said, "and because they knew my mother's father would never countenance such a marriage, they ... ran away together."

"That was brave of them."

"They were married in a small, obscure Church on the borders of Russia. Then they slipped into Poland and thought they were safe and could live happily ever afterwards."

Alana's voice broke on the last words and the Prince asked:

"What happened?"

"I suppose my mother was not aware of it, but after your father left Russia, Tzar Nicholas had put a complete and absolute ban on any Katinouskis ever leaving the country again. If they tried to do so, he ordered the Secret Police to follow them and bring them back to stand trial or, if they resisted, kill them!"

The Prince sat up abruptly in his chair.

"I had no idea of this. Why was my father not assassinated?"

"Perhaps your father was too important, too rich, and had too many distinguished European friends,"

148

Alana answered. "But my father and mother were in a very different category. They learnt through a Russian friend who was devoted to my mother that they were being sought by the Secret Police and the only way they could save themselves was by going into hiding."

The Prince's eyes expressed all too clearly that he knew what this meant.

"My father could not continue to play in the Orchestra, for they could go nowhere where they might be recognised," Alana went on. "For some years they lived in Holland, but as it became increasingly difficult to earn a living there, they went to Paris. It was only when Tzar Alexander showed himself not to be the despot and tyrant that Tzar Nicholas had been that they were brave enough to come to England. But they thought it was an unnecessary risk to live on my grandfather's Estates or to be too much in the company of the Wickhams."

"So they settled in Brilling!" the Prince said, as if he knew the end of the story.

"They came here," Alana said, "and my father gave music-lessons, and although they were poor they were very, very happy until my mother died."

"Just as we will be," the Prince said quietly.

Alana turned her face away as if she could not bear to look at him.

"There ... is something ... I have not ... told you," she said.

"What is that?"

"Under the edict of Tzar Nicholas, the marriage was annulled! The ceremony was declared ... null and ... void, and the Priest who ... conducted it was put to ... death!"

She paused before she said in a very different tone of voice:

"When I was ... born, I was ... therefore ... illegitimate!"

There was silence, and Alana turned from her contemplation of the fire to walk across the room and stand at the window.

She pulled back the curtains. Outside, there was darkness.

"Y-you now . . . understand," she said in a whisper, "why I cannot . . . marry you . . . or anyone else . . . I have no name . . . no real . . . identity!"

Chapter Seven

"Thank You, God...thank You...thank You!" Alana repeated over and over again to herself as, having been awakened by the singing of the gondoliers, she realised that the sun had risen and the canals were beginning to be busy.

It seemed more and more impossible every day to realise how fortunate she was as her happiness grew until like the sunshine it seemed to fill the whole world.

Yet it was true. She was married and the man sleeping beside her was her husband, to whom she belonged not only in name but with her whole being.

Every moment they were together she found it difficult to believe that they could in fact be closer.

Yet as each day of their honeymoon passed, she knew they were no longer two people but one, and their bodies, their minds, their hearts, and their souls had become indivisible one from the other.

Now in the great carved and painted Venetian bed which stood in the beautiful bedroom of one of the oldest and most magnificent Palazzos in Venice, Alana tried to express the gratitude in her

Barbara Cartland

heart and knew it would take her all her life to do so.

When she had told the Prince the secret of her birth, which she had felt was a wound inflicted deep into herself and which time would never heal, she had thought as she spoke the very word "illegitimate" that he would turn away from her in disgust.

She had known, she thought, even when she was small that it was a stigma both in Holland and in France, but as she grew older in England she was aware with what contempt the English, if they were kindly, referred to "love-children," and to "bastards" if they were not.

It was not known in Brilling that her father and mother were not legally married and therefore it did not trouble them, but Alana sometimes felt as if she were branded on her forehead for all to see.

When her mother had died, her father had put on her gravestone the words:

NATASHA, THE BELOVED AND ADORED WIFE
OF IRVING WICKHAM

"It is not true," Alana had said to him once. "Your marriage was annulled and therefore Mama was not your wife."

"To me she was not only my wife but everything that I worshipped, everything that gave me happiness," her father had replied firmly.

Then as if Alana had asked the question he added:

"She told me she never regretted running away with me from all the luxury and importance that was hers in Russia, and I believed her."

It was true, Alana thought.

Her mother had been completely happy and wherever they lived, the place radiated with love.

But Alana had told herself, almost as soon as she

152

was old enough to think, that she would never know the same happiness, for she could never be married.

What man would take as his wife a woman without a name? And, she added bitterly: "Someone who is repudiated both by the Russians and by the English."

She supposed that because she was young and impressionable, the years when they were in hiding had made her extremely sensitive to what other people were thinking and saying.

She knew that the English at any rate thought it strange that Mr. Wickham appeared to have no relations and that her mother, who was obviously a foreigner, never spoke of the land of her birth or admitted she had any nationality other than that of her husband.

It was only when eventually it percolated through to the quiet serenity of Brilling that the new Tzar, Alexander II, was different from the old one, that Irving Wickham became less worried that they might be found by the Secret Police.

When they learnt of the emancipation of the Serfs, and later the reforms that Alexander was bringing to his long-suffering country, Alana thought that a burden was lifted from her father's shoulders.

He no longer greeted every stranger with a searching look as if he was suspicious of his intentions.

But even if the Secret Police no longer sought them out, the stigma of her birth was still there; she was a child born out of wedlock, a child who grew into womanhood feeling that there was no society anywhere in which she could take her rightful place.

When she had said in a trembling voice to the Prince: "I have no name . . . no real identity," she had thought that the whole room was silent as if she had shocked the very atmosphere.

Then as she stood with her eyes shut, thinking that the Prince would turn and walk out of her life and she would never see him again, she heard him move, but towards her.

He came and stood beside her at the window and said:

"Before I tell you something that you should know, I want you to say quite simply that you believe our love is greater than anything else in the whole world."

The way he spoke seemed to vibrate through her and she could not answer, and after a moment he went on:

"To me it is greater than the laws of men, greater than any social code that was ever invented; it is in fact a love that is answerable only to God."

He paused before he added very softly:

"That is what I believe. Tell me, my darling, that you believe it too."

He was waiting, and she felt as though he commanded her to answer him until at last in a voice he could barely hear she murmured:

"I ... I love ... you! I love you ... desperately ... but ..."

Before she could say the last words, the Prince's arms were round her.

"That is all I want to hear," he said, "and that is all that matters."

He pulled her closer against him, then he tipped back her head and his lips were on hers.

He kissed her as he had before in the Music-Room, compellingly, fiercely, demandingly. She felt now as if masterfully he took her into his keeping, telling her without words that she could never escape him again.

He kissed her until they were no longer on earth but high in the sky and the glory of the light that enveloped them was Divine and yet came from within themselves.

It was so perfect and so sacred that Alana felt she must have died and was in Heaven.

Then as she felt as if they were surrounded with the music from a celestial choir, the very rapture of its spirituality broke under the strain, and as the Prince's lips became more passionate, Alana felt the flame of desire rise within her to meet the fire in him.

It was so wonderful and at the same time so beautiful that she could not think but only feel that this was love in all its majesty, omnipotent, unconquerable, and irresistible.

When at last the Prince raised his head, she could only hide her face against his neck and know that she vibrated to him as if she were a musical instrument in a master-hand.

Yet she knew that the melody he aroused in her was something so personal, so intimate that only he could understand what she was feeling.

"I love you, my darling," he said in a voice that was curiously unsteady. "I love and adore you, and we will be married immediately because I cannot live without you."

"H-how can you ... marry me?" Alana managed to gasp. "You know it is not ... right when you are ... of such importance."

"The only thing I consider of importance is you, but because it will make you happy I am going to tell you, my precious one, that your fears, which I know have hurt and distressed you all these years, are quite unfounded."

Alana raised her head.

"Unfounded?"

He held her a little closer to him as he said:

"I cannot bear to think that you have been worried and distressed quite unnecessarily because of that monster Tzar Nicholas, but the evil that men do does not always live after them."

"What are you ... saying?" Alana asked. "Explain to me ... I do not ... understand."

"You are not illegitimate, my darling," the Prince said, "but I promise you that even if you were, your identity would be very real to me."

"But ... Papa and Mama's marriage was ... annulled," Alana protested.

"It was one of the monstrous, insane acts of a tyrant," the Prince said, "but twelve or perhaps thirteen years ago, my father received a letter from Tzar Alexander asking him to return to Russia. He was promised that if he would do so, the lands he had owned would be restored to him and he would be welcomed at Court as his forebears had been for many generations."

The Prince spoke slowly, his eyes on Alana's face.

"In the same letter," he went on, "the Tzar said that all punishments, penalties, and privations directed against the Katinouskis during the last reign had been revoked and, where possible, the victims would be reinstated and compensated for their sufferings."

The Prince saw a sudden light come into Alana's eyes as she understood what he was saying.

To make it very clear, he added softly:

"That means, my precious love, that your father and mother's marriage was legal and that you were born in wedlock."

Alana gave a little cry of sheer happiness.

Her face was radiant, as if transformed by a light within her.

"Is ... that true ... really ... true?"

"I promise you it is," the Prince answered.

"If only Papa could have known that he need no longer be in hiding, that there was no longer the fear of Mama being taken back to Russia for punishment or killed if she refused to go!"

"The past cannot be undone," the Prince said quietly, "but the future is ours, Heart of my Heart."

His lips were on Alana's again and she felt there was a new rapture, a new wonder now in the feelings he evoked in her because she need no longer fight against her love for him.

After that, everything had happened with a swiftness that left her breathless.

The Prince had fetched her the next day from the Vicarage and they had travelled first to London, where they were married very quietly with no witnesses except for the Prince's Comptroller, then they had set out immediately to travel across Europe to Venice.

Alana half-suspected that one of the reasons for such haste was that the Prince had no wish to be involved in explanations to Lady Odele or to anybody else.

That was, however, a very small part of what she knew was a raging desire to have her alone and tell her of his love as he insisted she must tell him of hers.

Because, as he had said himself, he always got exactly what he wanted, there were no obstacles in his way, nor would he allow her to raise any.

Clothes appeared for her as if by magic, even before she had begun to think that she might seem like the beggar-maid whom King Cophetua had taken as his bride.

It was not only a question of being rich. She knew it was also because the Prince's life was so amazingly well organised and also because he was determined to make her happy.

When they arrived in London, she found that he had already sent a Courier ahead of them to have not only a wedding-gown and many other clothes waiting for her at his house but also jewellery such as she felt must have come from some Aladdin's cave.

After their marriage, there was the Prince's private train to take them to Dover, the Prince's yacht to carry them across the Channel, and again a private train in which they crossed France and Italy in such comfort and luxury that she was sure she was in a fairy-story.

"This cannot be true! I am dreaming!" Alana said to herself not once but a hundred times a day.

Yet when the Prince's arms were round her and his lips were on hers, she knew it was very real that she was his wife.

She found that Venice was as magical as she had expected.

They had arrived late in the evening and had dined in a room that was redolent with history.

But it was hard to think of anything except the Prince's eyes looking into hers and the note in his voice, which made her feel that she responded to a melody which came from the stars overhead.

After he had made love to her gently, but arousing her spiritually and physically to new sensations she had not known existed, she had gone to sleep in his arms.

Yet, even as she slept, she held on to him for fear that in the morning she would wake and find he had vanished.

But he was there beside her and there was the song of the gondoliers and the golden sunshine percolating through the curtains which she knew hid one of the most beautiful views in the world.

"I am in Venice . . . I am married, and Ivan . . . loves me!" Alana's heart was singing. "Thank You, God . . . oh, thank You!"

As if the very intensity of her prayer communicated itself to the Prince, he opened his eyes and in the dim light saw her face near to his.

There was a sudden warmth in his expression as he smiled.

He reached out and his arms drew her closer to him. Her body was very soft and yielding against his and he asked:

"Why are you awake, my beautiful darling?"

"I do not wish to . . . waste time in sleeping when I am . . . here with . . . you."

The way she spoke told the Prince a great deal more than the words she actually said, and after a moment of sheer happiness he asked:

"What are you thinking?"

"I am saying a . . . prayer of . . . gratitude."

"I thought that was what you were doing, and it is something I must do too, because I have found the woman I have been seeking all my life but thought did not actually exist."

"And now you . . . know I . . . do?"

"I am not only grateful," the Prince replied, "but very excited."

His lips moved against her skin and his hand was touching her.

"Oh, Ivan," Alana cried, "how could I ever have known or guessed, when I was so glad to find work at the Vicarage after Papa died, that I would ever be married to you and be living in such beautiful places as this?"

"Which is the most important?" the Prince asked teasingly.

"You . . . only you!"

He would have kissed her lips, but she said in a low voice:

"I was thinking last night just before I went to sleep that if through any unforeseen change in your fortune you had to go into exile like Papa and Mama and hide from the Secret Police, I would go with you not only willingly but . . . gladly."

"Gladly?" the Prince questioned.

"I could then make you understand that I love you . . . only for . . . yourself and not for . . . anything you possess or any position you hold."

She gave a little sigh as if it was difficult to find words before she went on:

"It is . . . wonderful, very . . . very . . . wonderful to be the wife of somebody who is treated almost like a King . . . who can have anything he wishes . . . and who owns so many marvellous things. But it is all completely unimportant beside you . . . the real . . . you."

The Prince did not speak and she looked at him with a worried expression in her eyes before she said:

"You do understand . . . you do believe that what I am telling you is the . . . truth?"

"My precious, my beautiful darling!" the Prince replied. "Of course I believe what you are saying to me, but it is quite unnecessary. My instinct tells me far better than words that you love me as I want to be loved, and I know I shall spend every day of my life trying to make you understand what I feel for you."

"I have . . . an instinct . . . too."

"I know that," the Prince replied tenderly, "but it does not always work when you are thinking of yourself."

He knew she was waiting for him to explain, and he went on:

"When I came into the Nursery and saw you bathing the baby, I was aware that you were shy and a little embarrassed at my finding you performing such a menial task, but, my beautiful sweetheart, if you had only known what it meant for me to see you and know that all my fortune could not buy what you typified at that moment."

"I thought once," Alana said in a low voice, "that all your . . . fine houses, since you were alone and had no ... children, were ... none of them a ... home."

"That is what I realised," the Prince said, "when I saw you looking so utterly adorable and very feminine with that small boy on your lap."

He hesitated a moment before he said:

"My mother was a cold woman, or so she seemed to me. Perhaps that is a love I have missed in my life, and I know too that I have missed having brothers and sisters, who would have loved me because I belonged to them."

"Oh, darling, I understand," Alana cried, "but wherever we are, I can make a home for you and I will give you children to ... make up for the loneliness that you must have felt being an only child ... as I was."

"That is what I want, Light of my Life," the Prince said, "and I know that we will never allow our children to feel unloved or that they have to fight against their instinct as I have done."

"You are not ... fighting against it ... now?"

He knew the question was important, and he replied:

"Not since you prevented me from doing so. Now I can love you unreservedly and use every instinct in my body and my soul to give you all the happiness you deserve."

"You are so ... so ... wonderful!" Alana cried. "How could I have ever imagined there was a man like you in the world or that I would be lucky enough to find him?"

"That is what I thought when I found you."

"That is not true!" Alana retorted. "You told me yourself you were afraid and you tried to run away from me."

"I should have known it would be impossible," the Prince said. "We have between us a power so strong and so irresistible that it can never be denied."

"You are sure of that?" Alana asked. "I am a little ... afraid that one day you might want to revert to being ... completely English, and then you will no longer ... want me."

The Prince smiled.

"Do you really think that possible when we are so close that if I lost you I should lose half of myself? And I think you would say the same. We are one, Alana, joined by the power we felt pouring towards us from the Ikons, the power which in some strange, mysterious way brought us together in this life as we have been together in other lives."

"That is what I want to believe. Oh, Ivan, I love you! It is difficult to find words to tell you how much ... so I can only go on saying, 'I love you!' and give you my soul ... my very ... Russian soul!"

"I adore you, I worship you," the Prince murmured. "I want to kneel at your feet and light candles to the holiness of you."

"Ivan! Ivan! I am so afraid I shall ... fail you!"

"How could you do that when you are purity personified, the Ikon my soul has sought since the beginning of time!"

"I love ... you!"

He was kissing her neck, her shoulders, and her breasts, and as she stirred against him he said:

"I want to take the stars and weave them into a chain to bind you to me. I want to imprison you in the moon so that no man may see your beauty, which is mine."

"Darling, there is no need for chains or prisons. I am yours ... completely and ... absolutely."

Alana's voice was passionate with the intensity of what she was saying and because the Prince's mouth and hands were making her quiver with a rising excitement.

He gave a laugh that was one of sheer happiness. Then he was kissing her passionately, demanding that she surrender herself to him with a masterfulness against which she had no defence.

She felt the fire that burned in his eyes rise like a flame within her breasts.

Once again, as always when the Prince made love to her, she heard music in the air and felt the vibrations of the light coming from within themselves to join with the light which came from the Divine.

Then there was only love, the vivid, compelling, mysterious power of love, for which there are no words.

ABOUT THE AUTHOR

BARBARA CARTLAND, the world's most famous romantic novelist, who is also an historian, playwright, lecturer, political speaker and television personality, has now written over 200 books.

She has also had many historical works published and has written four autobiographies as well as the biographies of her mother and that of her brother Ronald Cartland, who was the first Member of Parliament to be killed in the last war. This book has a preface by Sir Winston Churchill.

Barbara Cartland has sold 100 million books over the world, more than half of these in the U.S.A. She broke the world record in 1975 by writing twenty books, and her own record in 1976 with twenty-one. In addition, her album of love songs has just been published, sung with the Royal Philharmonic Orchestra.

In private life, Barbara Cartland, who is a Dame of the Order of St. John of Jerusalem, has fought for better conditions and salaries for Midwives and Nurses. As President of the Royal College of Midwives (Hertfordshire Branch), she has been invested with the first Badge of Office ever given in Great Britain which was subscribed to by the Midwives themselves. She has also championed the cause for old people and founded the first Romany Gypsy Camp in the world.

Barbara Cartland is deeply interested in Vitamin Therapy and is President of the British National Association for Health.

Barbara Cartland

The world's bestselling author of romantic fiction. Her stories are always captivating tales of intrigue, adventure and love.

☐	12572	THE DRUMS OF LOVE	$1.50
☐	12576	ALONE IN PARIS	$1.50
☐	12638	THE PRINCE AND THE PEKINGESE	$1.50
☐	12637	A SERPENT OF SATAN	$1.50
☐	12273	THE TREASURE IS LOVE	$1.50
☐	12785	THE LIGHT OF THE MOON	$1.50
☐	12792	PRISONER OF LOVE	$1.50
☐	12281	FLOWERS FOR THE GOD OF LOVE	$1.50
☐	13391	THE EXPLOSION OF LOVE	$1.50

Barbara Cartland

The world's bestselling author of romantic fiction. Her stories are always captivating tales of intrigue, adventure and love.

Bantam Book Catalog

Here's your up-to-the-minute listing of over 1,400 titles by your favorite authors.

This illustrated, large format catalog gives a description of each title. For your convenience, it is divided into categories in fiction and non-fiction—gothics, science fiction, westerns, mysteries, cookbooks, mysticism and occult, biographies, history, family living, health, psychology, art.

So don't delay—take advantage of this special opportunity to increase your reading pleasure.

Just send us your name and address and 50¢ (to help defray postage and handling costs).